A SUMMER TO REMEMBER WITH MY HITTA

NAI

URBAN AINT DEAD PRESENTS

URBAN AINT DEAD
P.O Box 960780
Riverdale GA., 30296

Cover Design: P. Wise / The Wise Services

Edited By: Veronica Rena Miller / Red Diamond Editing by V. Rena, LLC
reddiamondediting5@yahoo.com

URBAN AINT DEAD and coinciding logo(s) are registered properties.

Contact Author on FB: Authoress Nai / IG: @authoressnai / TikTok: @authoressnai

Contact Publisher at www.urbanaintdead.com

Email: urbanaintdead@gmail.com

Print ISBN: 979-8-9904701-5-6

Scan the QR Code below to listen to the Soundtracks/Singles of some of your favorite U.A.D titles:

Don't have Spotify or Apple Music?
No Sweat!
Visit your choice streaming platform and search URBAN AINT DEAD.

Currently on lock serving a bid?
JPay, iHeartRadio, WHATEVER!
We got you covered.
Simply log into your facility's kiosk or tablet, go to music and search URBAN AINT DEAD.

URBAN AINT DEAD

Like & Follow us on social media:

FB – URBAN AINT DEAD

IG: @urbanaintdead

Tik Tok - @urbanaintdead

SUBMISSION GUIDELINES

Submit the first three chapters of your completed manuscript to urbanaintdead@gmail.com, subject line: Your book's title. The manuscript must be in a .doc file and sent as an attachment. The document should be in Times New Roman, double-spaced, and in size 12 font. Also, provide your synopsis and full contact information. If sending multiple submissions, they must each be in a separate email. Have a story but no way to submit it electronically? You can still submit to URBAN AINT DEAD. Send in the first three chapters, written or typed, of your completed manuscript to:

URBAN AINT DEAD
P.O Box 960780
Riverdale GA., 30296

DO NOT send original manuscript. Must be a duplicate.
Provide your synopsis and a cover letter containing your full contact information.

Thanks for considering URBAN AINT DEAD.

CHAPTER ONE – CHARISMA

I DON'T WANNA BE YOUR GIRLFRIEND, I'M JUST TRYNA BE YOUR PERSON. I don't need to be your girl, uh, cool with just being your person.

I sang Sza's "Notice Me" as I got ready for my 9 a.m. shift at the Lexus dealership. I'd been working as the front desk receptionist for the last year and a half, and I loved it. It paid well and it gave me the flexibility I needed for my school schedule. Being in school full time for social work was no joke. The late-night study sessions and long class schedules were enough to make me hang it up, but I had goals, and I was going to accomplish them.

I'd surprised myself when I made it to my one-year anniversary at my job. I was known to get the fuck on if a job didn't suit me. I know, it sounds crazy, and maybe a little irresponsible to some, but hey, life was too short to be miserable and unhappy working for someone else. Shit, the 19 taught me that; covid-19 that was.

I hit my body with a few sprays of Valentino perfume and disconnected my phone from my Bluetooth system. Grabbing my keys and purse from the dresser, I kissed my beautiful reflection that stared back at me in the mirror and was ready to take on the day. Summer had officially kicked off, and I was more than happy to pull out my array of maxi dresses. Today's color was yellow, and the bright color went well with my golden, bronze skin tone. Standing at 5'2", I considered myself slim thick.

Double D cup breasts sat up on my chest, followed by a small waist, and a juicy ass that had a matching thigh ratio. Yes, a bad bitch by any man's or woman's standard. Top that off with the fact that I was book smart; that translated to *unfuckwitable* in all languages. Knowing the 65 degree temp they kept the air on at the dealership, I grabbed a jean jacket from my closet.

Ensuring that all of my electronics were unplugged and put away, I made my way out front. As I prepared to leave my apartment, a loud thud up against my front door made me jump back. Now, I was known to go toe to toe with the best of them, but I wasn't stupid. Whatever was going on on the other side of the door, I wanted no parts of. So, I decided to wait it out and be nosey at the same time.

"Why the fuck you got me chasing you down like I'm some bill collector, Jay?" I heard a male's voice say before hearing another loud thud followed by groaning.

"It ain't like that, man." I placed another male's voice but this one was weak. It let me know that he was the reason for the banging against the door and likely the groan came from him. *"Le said she paid you."*

"Did Le borrow that bread from me, Jay?" The aggressor questioned. The weakened male stayed silent, and I wanted him to respond so bad cause I could tell that the aggressor wasn't playing at all. *"Did she?"*

"Nah, Has."

"Aight, then. Don't send nobody my way with excuses to pay off your debts. Have the rest of my bread in the next hour or my next stop is gonna be one of your family members' cribs. And don't ask me for shit else, Jay. I wouldn't care if yo ass was on fire and my call to the fire department could save you. DON'T ASK ME FOR SHIT!"

"My bad, Has," he responded, pathetically.

"You got an hour, nigga. And you already know how I play. Get the fuck up!"

His demand scared me, and I waited for about a minute before going to the peephole to see if I was in the clear to leave. Looking out, I could see a hooded man standing in front of the door with his head down.

"What the hell?" I yelled out, jumping back for the second time.

"Sorry bout your door, shorty," the guy offered. "Here's something to get it fixed."

"Wait, what?" I snatched my door open just as he was kneeling down to slide a few bills under it. "Excuse me?" I spoke to the top of his head. Turning slightly, I gasped, taking note of the dent in the door. "Are you serious?"

He stood on his feet and pulled his hoody back enough for me to see his face. He easily towered over my 5'2 frame, standing at at least 5'7. His skin was the color of butterscotch candy. He had the face of a fifteen-year-old but his eyes were dark, indicating he'd lived a life or was currently living one. All in all, he was very handsome. The only blemish on his face was a small scar under his left eye.

"I said, my bad," he spoke, his voice filled with annoyance, breaking my concentration. In my head, I'd traced his jaw line with my French tips.

"How you gon' have an attitude about some shit that was your fault?"

"Look, 2A, you want the bread or not? I got shit to do." He held up four one-hundred-dollar bills.

"Who the hell is 2..." I stopped and concluded that he was referring to my apartment number. "Just give me the money. If my landlord tries to start some shit with me because of this, I'm coming to look for you."

"And if I wanna be found, you'll find me, 2A. Again, I apologize. Have a good day." Pulling his hoodie back forward, he pulled up his pants and swaggered off. My eyes were glued to his back as he made his way to the stairway door and walked through it to likely ruin someone else's day.

"Unfuckinbelieveable," I said aloud. Shaking my head, I stepped out into the hallway, closing and locking my door behind me. Sliding the bills the babyface thug had given me into my purse, I made my way to the elevator.

I couldn't have imagined that this would be the start of my morning. I just hoped that my annoying ass landlord didn't trip when he saw the damage. I mean, it wasn't crazy, but it was damn sure noticeable.

By the time I made it outside to my car it was 8:15 a.m. I'd still make it to work on time, but I'd have little wiggle room. Hopping in my car, I turned the air on full blast and went to shift into drive when I saw Babyface exiting my building.

I watched him get into the passenger seat of a double parked S500 and thought, *"Damn, Babyface, why you couldn't be getting into the driver's seat?"* Quickly snapping back into the reality that Babyface's business wasn't my business, I pulled off on a mission to not break my perfect attendance record.

———

MY DAY AT WORK SEEMED TO END JUST AS IT STARTED; THAT'S HOW fast the time flew by. The customers had been in and out all day, keeping me busy and I welcomed the pace. Shutting down and restarting my computer for the next workday, I went to grab my purse and a bottled water when I heard my name called. Looking up from my desk, I found my manager walking in my direction accompanied by the owner of the dealership. I couldn't read their facial expressions from the distance. I don't know why but as they made their way over, I felt a little anxious. Taking a deep breath, I spoke.

"Hey, Chelsea, hey, Andrew." My greeting was light and airy just as it normally was.

"Hey, Charisma. Are you headed out for the day?" Andrew questioned.

"I am. Did you need something?"

"Actually, yes," Chelsea spoke. "Do you mind coming to my office?"

I squinted my eye trying to get a good read on the situation but again, I didn't pick up on anything. "Chelsea, if y'all plan on firing me, I'd much rather y'all go ahead and do it now where I'm close to the exit. It'll make the distance for my walk of shame that much shorter."

"Charisma, we are not firing you." Chelsea giggled and I did the same to mask my relief. "It's a good thing, I promise."

"Okay," I let out, "after you." She proceeded to walk in front of me while Andrew gestured for me to walk ahead of him.

The white boy clearly wanted a view of my perfect round ass. He knew damn well he could've walked behind Chelsea. Entering the office, Andrew closed the door behind us, and Chelsea stood on the side of her desk. Andrew chose to sit partially on the edge of it.

"First, I wanna say thank you for all that you do daily when it comes to the business. Your hard work doesn't go unnoticed." Hearing Chelsea big me up in front of her boss made me smile.

I knew I did my job well but to have my boss brag on me in front of the owner was top tier. "Thank you, Chelsea. I appreciate that."

"Yes," Andrew added, "Chelsea has mentioned your name in almost every staff meeting over the last six months. And for this one to mention you," he pointed to Chelsea, "it really means something. Which is why we brought you in here today. You may not know it, but it seems that you've been responsible for a few car sales here lately. Customers have raved about your customer service and the overall vibe you bring to the showroom floor. So much so that you've been able to persuade some of our most indecisive customers into a purchase."

"Wow, really? So, is it safe to say that y'all owe me a lil' commission change?"

They both got a good laugh out of my comment, clearly not catching onto the fact that I was deadass serious. I kept the smile on my face, though.

"I see why the customers love you so much. How would you feel if we offered you the opportunity to make more money?" Andrew asked.

"I'm all ears."

"We'd like you to try your hand at sales."

"You mean like selling cars?"

"Yep."

"Umm, I never thought about it."

"I think you'd be great at it," Chelsea cosigned. "You wanna give it some thought? There's no rush for an answer right this minute."

I paused before responding. I already knew my answer was, no. I didn't see selling cars in my future. However, I still appreciated them considering me, so I opted to let them down easy by telling them I'd think about it.

"Give me a day or two to wrap my head around it," I said.

"Sounds fair." Andrew stood and held his hand out for me to shake. I accepted his gesture, and we shook on it.

"Have a goodnight, Charisma." Chelsea gave me a smile and wink as I turned to leave.

"You too, Chelsea." I left her office, grabbed my belongings, and headed for my car thinking, *yousa bad bitch, Charisma Dalton.*

CHAPTER TWO – HASAN

"WHAT THAT NIGGA, JAY, TALKIN' BOUT?" MY BOY, BOOGIE, ASKED as I jumped in his passenger seat.

"Shit, I did most of the talkin'," I replied. "It wasn't much I was willing to hear after the nigga went MIA for a week knowing he owed me bread. He lucky I didn't close casket his ass."

"That shit wouldn't have made you feel no better, and you still wouldn't have yo bread, playboy."

"Yeah, I think his head bouncing off a few doors up there gave him the push he needed. I told him he had an hour to get my money to me."

Boogie chuckled and shook his head. "And so, we wait?"

"We wait," I repeated. Pulling my phone from my pocket, I went through my notifications to check my text messages.

Checking the time on the phone, I yawned. These weren't my normal hours to run the streets, but a nigga that had me fucked up made it so that I was up at seven this morning and in the hood by eight. Everyone who came in contact with me knew I didn't play about my time. It was the one thing we couldn't get back. I'd fucked around and gone against my own rule and let one of my childhood friends borrow some bread to get him out of a jam. Somewhere along the way, this nigga had taken my kindness for sweetness cause the deadline to return said bread had come and gone. And here I was having to threaten a nigga behind my shit.

As I scrolled through my messages, swiping pass the ones who didn't need an immediate response, I came up on an unread message from my daughter's mother, Heather. She'd texted me early this morning and being that I was on the move, I'd marked it unread to go back to. I knew it wasn't anything important regarding our daughter because Heather knew to call my phone if it had anything to do with Bella and her well-being.

Bella was two years old and had come in and hijacked my heart from the moment she was born. August 2nd, 2021, she entered this world and became the highlight of my existence. With a cute round face, chubby cheeks, almond shaped eyes, and a head full of thick, curly hair that her mother kept in a cute style with the help of YouTube and TikTok. My daughter was everything. If me and Heather did anything right during our relationship, we could put creating the perfect little human to the top of the list. Clicking on her audio message, I put my phone up to my ear to listen.

"Hey, Hasan, I was just reaching out to see if you were still picking Bella up tomorrow night. It's no pressure, I just wanted to confirm. If you have business to handle, I completely understand. Just let me know. Oh, and I was thinking, maybe on Sunday, we could have a little family day. You know, take Bella on a little picnic or something."

The message ended and I sighed before texting my response. This was the downside to my co-parenting relationship with Heather. While I had long ago accepted that our romantic relationship was over, she was still holding onto this idea of us being a family. When I wanted to do the family thing, she was more focused on the time I spent in the street than cultivating our relationship. With as much havoc as I wreaked in the streets on the daily, Heather couldn't grasp the fact that I wanted to come home to peace, not a full-on interrogation about where I'd been all day.

I was a provider mentally, physically, and emotionally. I took care of our home and before Bella made her debut, I made sure Heather was taking care of. All I asked was that she made sure she had a life outside of me. That way when I was in the streets, she could keep herself occupied as well. She wasn't trying to hear that. A loner by choice, in her head, all she had was me. Tired of feeling stifled after a while, I bowed out gracefully and continued to be the best father to our child just as my father had been to me before he was killed.

"It's too damn hot to be sitting out here for an hour, bruh," Boogie complained. I knew it was coming.

"Turn the ac back on then. You the only nigga I know who drive around in a luxury car and don't use all of its functions."

"Nigga, gas is twenty dollars a gallon out this bitch. I ain't bout to keep my shit running for no hour and we sitting still."

"Well then, be hot, nigga."

"Says the crazy dude with the hoody on."

I looked down at my Balenciaga hoodie and shrugged my shoulders. Texting Heather back, I assured her that I would be at her house tomorrow to get my baby, I chose not to address the family picnic invitation. I didn't wanna give any false hope.

"Shit, Jay must've known you wasn't fucking around," Boogie let out, tapping my arm, and pointing at the window.

Jay made his way up the block, his steps intentional. He'd cleaned up his face and gone was the slight limp he had when he'd ran off earlier. Recognizing Boogie's car, Jay continued in our direction. Before he could walk up to the passenger side where I was seated, Boogie beeped the horn.

"Hurry up, nigga, it's hot!" He barked from his open window.

Jay nodded and came over to me. I rolled the window down just as he was digging in his pocket. He pulled out a knot of cash, wrapped in a rubber band.

"Fuck is this, sneaker box money? What you think we in the 80's, nigga?" He extended his hand to give me the money and I snatched it from him. Normally, I gave everyone respect, but tryna run off with my bread was disrespectful so me snatching the money was warranted.

"It's all there, man," he said, watching me unwrap the bills and began counting them.

"Yeah, that may be the case but after recent events, it's better to be safe than sorry. I'm gonna be safe so you don't have to be sorry, feel me." I had half a mind to count the bills real slow, but I didn't wanna keep Boogie longer than I had to. I counted out the knot of twenties and a few singles. Once I confirmed that it equaled the $2,500 he owed, I sat the money in my lap. "So that we're clear, we ain't homies, friends, associates, none of that shit no more. You go yo way and I go mine. And I hope for yo sake that you never need a nigga again." Without giving him a chance to respond, I rolled the window up and signaled for Boogie to pull off.

"We going to see Unc?" Boogie inquired while turning onto the 145th street bridge to take us into the Bronx.

"Yeah. He say he need to holla at us about something."

Whatever it was that Uncle Myles needed to talk to us about, I knew there was money involved. Uncle Myles was about his paper. He was my father's younger brother, his only living sibling. My grandparents were deceased, and my dad was killed in a drug deal that went left. My mother was, well, she was my mother. Uncle Myles had been raising me ever since my dad had been killed. Not because my mother wasn't around, she was.

In fact, she was a great mother up until my father died. I knew when he died, he took apart of her with him, making it hard for her to continue to be a mother to me. At thirteen years old, she dropped me off at my uncle's crib and I remembered her words verbatim. *"My husband died by your hands and I can't raise a young, black man in this world today so the least you can do is pick up where big Hasan left off."* She kissed my cheek and though I wanted to cry, I held in it. I didn't have any hard feelings then and I didn't have any when she showed back up two years later after limited contact with me.

Her absence shaped the man I was today, and I was still trying to figure out if that was a good or bad thing. In my quest to figure that out, I kept her at a distance, reasoning that I had to love her because she was my mom, but also understanding that we no longer had the capacity to embrace each other the way we had when my father was alive. It was safe to say that Unc was the only parental figure I really acknowledged.

"Aye, you think you can line my shit up for me later? I'm taking my shorty out on a date later."

"What shorty, nigga?" I tucked the money away in my pants pocket and waited for Boogie to tell me some bullshit.

"The shorty I'm taking out later. Get you one."

"Ahhh, aight. It's one of them lil' sluts you fuck with. Man, you don't need no lineup, you know the chicken heads don't require much." He glanced in my direction, and we were both quiet before cracking up laughing.

"Don't talk about my shorty like that," he chuckled. "She ain't like them other bitches. I might let her spend the night at my...hotel room."

Still laughing, I shook my head. "Aight, I got you. Soon you gon' have to start paying me. All these free cuts bout to be ova when I open up the shop."

"Yeah, yeah, holla at me when you get that shop, bruh. Until then, line a nigga up."

He didn't know it yet, but I planned on making that dream a reality soon.

———

"WASSUP WITH IT, UNC?" BOTH ME AND BOOGIE ENTERED THE sports bar my uncle owned and dapped him up. The bar was used for business meetings during the day and at night, it was one of the littest places in the Bronx. Unc knew how to make some money, both the legal and illegal way. He just so happened to like the latter more.

"What's good y'all? Have a seat. Y'all had breakfast yet?" He closed his Daily News and set it down next to him on the bar's countertop.

"I'm good. You know this dude a breakfast burrito away from being Biggie Smalls," I pointed at Boogie. "I'm sure he wants something."

"Shut up, nigga. Ms. Bonnie back there?"

"Yeah. She's prepping for the brunch we're hosting this afternoon. Go back there and see what she can whip up for you, Boog."

Boogie took the hint that Unc wanted to talk to me alone and went off to the back.

"What you got for me?"

"How you been, Has?" This was usually how our conversations about business started off before he ran down what needed to be done. He always wanted to check my temperature.

"You know we do this every time, right? I'm good, Unc. In fact, I'm great. I'm always great."

He turned his body so that he was fully facing me and for a moment, I thought back to the one on one's I used to have with my father. Uncle Myle's and my father could've easily passed for twins.

"I check in with you to see where yo head at cause you my left hand, and I know the tasks I set before you aren't ones that don't require some kind of emotion."

"I'm straight, Unc. What you got for me?"

He nodded. "There's a party here tonight. I need you to have a one on one with the host." He paused and took a sip from his coffee cup. "He owes me something and that sudden case of amnesia made him think it was okay to host a party as opposed to settling his debt."

"You mean to tell me this nigga owe you some bread and he coming here to party? He don't know you own this shit?"

Unc shrugged while pushing his chair out to stand. "Most people don't...and I like it that way. Be here by midnight to take care of that."

"I'm on it. We making an example or you want it quiet?"

"Use your discretion, Has. Whatever you decide, clean-up will be on standby, and Toni will be here to shut down. Cool?"

"Cool." We dapped each other up and embraced in a manly hug.

"If you have Bella this weekend, bring her by the house so she can get in the pool. Liv has been asking for her." Liv was my uncle's girl-friend who was ten years his junior and had no kids of her own.

She took to Bella the first day meeting her and while Bella was a little hard on Liv at first, they now spent as much time together as me and Bella did. She was Bella's Nani, and that was cool with me. Although she wasn't my mother, we'd grown a bond over the last five years she'd been around.

"Aight."

"Thanks, Ms. B. You threw down on them French toast." Boogie emerged from the back where the kitchen was located and Ms. B was right behind him with a styrofoam container.

"You're welcome, Boog. Here you go, love." She handed me the container and pecked my cheek. "Y'all be safe out there and bring the little diva by soon, Has. I told her we could have a tea party next time I saw her."

"I'll have her this weekend. This little girl is busier than me. Everybody wanna see her."

Ms. B laughed and made her way back to the kitchen.

"I'm up, Unc. I'll catch you later."

"Eyes open, nephew," he said as me and Boogie made our exit.

"Even when I'm sleeping," I yelled back, pushing the door open.

"You putting in work tonight?" Boogie asked as we got back in the car.

I gave him a look of confirmation. Taking care of problems had been my job for the last eight years. When I told Unc I wanted in on the family business, he put a gun in my hand rather than a pack. He said he didn't need another hustler on the block. He needed someone he trusted with his life to watch his back and handle other business he didn't feel comfortable putting in a colleague's hand. Seeing that I knew my way around guns, putting me in the position was a no brainer. And for the last few years, I'd been the muscle; I took care of shit.

CHAPTER THREE – CHARISMA

"So, you really not gonna come out with us tonight?" My best friend, Brae'lynn, whined on the other end of the phone.

We'd been on the call for the last hour, and I was about to tell her no for the third time. I wasn't in the mood to hang out. I'd just finished a busy work week along with an intense study week. I was the definition of *tired*.

"Brae'lynn," I whined back, **"I don't feel like getting dressed up tonight. I'm curled up in my bed, in my pjs, and that's where I shall remain for the remainder of the night, watching reruns of *Martin*."**

"Ughh, you were never this boring. Girl, its summertime, and the niggas is out. Come outside and let's do bald head hoe shit." I laughed because I just knew she was twerking when she said that. **"And you just got a new job offer, we need to be out celebrating."**

I'd told her about my conversation with Chelsea and Andrew, now she was using it as a selling point. **"I told you I'm not taking the job."** Reaching over on my nightstand, I picked up my bottle of water that had the different times printed on the front of it to encourage my intake. I was well on my way to reaching my goal of drinking a gallon of water for the day.

"Girl, a win is a win. And now you know that your hard work isn't going unnoticed. I think that's something to celebrate. So, let's do that over a few shots, drinks, and some food. I'ma eat before I leave the house, though. That way I can drink more."

"Since when has shots and drinks not been the same damn thing, Brae'lynn? Not you becoming a functioning alcoholic." I snickered a little at my own joke.

"Oohh, that was a low blow and I'ma let you slide because I really want you to come outside tonight. Trust, we gon' spend back to the topic. Pleaseeeee, come out with us."

I blew out an exaggerated sigh and kissed my teeth. I'd known Brae'lynn for ten years and if I knew nothing else, I knew my friend was persistent. She was that way when it came to her whole approach to life. In her mind, persistence got you everywhere.

"Don't ask me to go out for the rest of the weekend, Brae'lynn."

"Ahhhhh," she squealed. **"Come on and put that shit on, booka. Let me call Asani and tell her that I wore you down. Sheesh! You made me work this time, heffa. A whole hour of begging. I'll be to you by ten so we can roll out, roll out."** She sang into the phone, expressing her excitement.

"Whatever. A minute after ten and the party fi dun."

"Alright, Sean Paul," she giggled. **"I'll see you at 9:59p.m. Love you."** Hanging up the phone, I shook my head and sighed.

Granted, I hadn't been out in a minute, but it was because my schedule didn't permit much leisure time. I was cool with that; wasn't shit outside for me no way. Setting my binder and textbook to the side, I got up to shower. Brae'lynn was a stickler for time, so 10p.m. for her was really 9:55p.m. The girl was punctual.

I adored my friends. They were both ambitious and goal driven like me. Brae'lynn was an RN and in the process of opening a juice bar alongside one of her coworkers. She was newly single and after coming from underneath her man's thumb, she'd embraced being outside. Asani was a Real Estate agent, slowly but surely making a name for herself with her unique way of marketing commercial spaces. She'd also recently inherited her family's daycare center that she operated behind the scenes.

Asani had taken on her new role with angst but after putting the right people in place, it freed up her time to continue to live her life as a jetsetter. The three of us were single with no children, and while the two of them didn't want any, I, on the other hand, wanted at least four. Growing up an only child was boring and often lonely. Yeah, I didn't have to share my toys but fighting over a toy with a sibling sounded way better than having imaginary friends. I wanted my kids two years apart in age, too. It was important that they grew up together and that they were close.

All in all, me, Asani, and Brae'lynn were a close-knit group. I liked it that way. For me, the less people you kept around, the chance of your business being in the street was low. Stepping out of the bed, I stretched my body and headed for the bathroom. Leaning over the bathroom sink, I talked to myself in the mirror.

"Alright now, Charisma, I know your body is tired, but you could use this night out. You have been in overdrive; you can let your hair down a little. Go out, have a drink or two, and have fun with your girls. If anybody deserves the break, it's you." Finishing up my pep talk, Babyface's face flashed in my head.

It was the second time today that he'd crossed my mind. There was something about his eyes that I couldn't get out of my head. The money he'd given me for my door was sitting on top of my bookshelf near the front door, waiting for the landlord. I still hadn't come up with a story to tell him of what had happened. I knew I wasn't gonna rat out, Babyface, though. My landlord was notorious for calling the cops over the smallest things. Hearing that someone had dented the door during an altercation was sure to send him running down to the precinct.

Placing the shower cap on my head, I stepped into the semi hot shower and let out a deep sigh. I let the water run over my body before washing and exfoliating. Between washing and my off-key singing, my normal shower routine took at least twenty minutes. For the sake of time, I cut it down to give myself time to get dressed. I stood in the middle of my closet for five minutes, mentally putting fits together in my head before remembering that I hadn't asked Brae'lynn where we were going. I sauntered back over to my bed and called out for Siri to call her. The call connected after the first ring.

"If you're calling to flake on me, you might as well hang up now cuz I ain't tryna hear it." She was either on the phone when I called or had anticipated that at some point I'd change my mind before she got to my house.

I giggled before speaking. **"I'm not flaking. I called to see where we were going tonight. I need to get an idea of what to wear."** Placing the phone on speaker, I returned to my closet.

"Oh, a coworker of mine invited me to a party at this sports bar in the Bronx."

"Eww, a sports bar?" The disdain in my tone couldn't be missed. **"Brae'lynn, do it look like I watch sports? Girl, you don't even watch sports. Had you led with that, I would've definitely told you no."** Rolling my eyes, I pouted and snatched a pair of ripped jean shorts off the hanger and pulled an oversize graphic tee from the dresser drawer.

"The fact that you think that I was going with sports in mind goes to show how much you know about your friend. And we don't have to stay long, just a quick scope of the crowd, one drink, and we can hit another spot. Plus, I heard it be poppin' in there; not your average sports bar."

"Yeah, well, unfortunately, I can't take your word for it. You know, since you haven't been there." Sarcasm dripped from my voice.

"So, cute/casual will work," she responded, ignoring me. **"Anything else, princess?"** It was her turn to be sarcastic now.

"No. I'm getting dressed now."

"Okay, see you in a few." In my frustration, I hung up before she did. Laying my clothes out on the bed, I dropped my phone next to them.

Brae'lynn knew exactly what she was doing. I was gonna let her slide this time even though everything in me was saying, "climb back in the bed." Trading my towel for my robe, I sat down at my vanity and commenced to applying light makeup to my face. I was no pro when it came to the makeup thing but with the tips I'd picked up from YouTube and the girlies on Tik Tok, I did my little one, two. I spent twenty minutes on that, applied a little setting spray, and moved onto hair next.

My sew-in was still intact from earlier, so a little refresh of my baby hairs and I was in the game. I'd managed to be fully dressed by 9:45 p.m. Feeling good about how everything had come together, I grabbed my Goyard handbag and tossed in my wallet, keys, hand sanitizer, a pack of gum, and my phone. There was a small pocketknife nestled in the bag as well. You could never be too careful out here.

I gave my body a few spritz of Burberry Her perfume, picked up my boots from where they sat by my room door, and made my way to the livingroom. Just as I went to sit down to put them on, my doorbell rang. I smiled because Brae'lynn was so predictable.

"Who is it?" I played while walking over to the door.

"The bestest friends in the whole wide world," Asani sang her response.

"Yeah, and one of them has to pee really bad, so open the door please," Brae'lynn followed up.

I opened the door and she practically ran pass me but stopped before making it to the bathroom. Kicking off her heels, she proceeded to rush to the back of my apartment.

"Thank you," I yelled out, closing the door behind Asani. I didn't play the shoes through my house thing. "Hey, boo. How was your day?" I asked her.

"Girl, hectic. I'm ready to get a drink in my system. What the hell happened to your door?"

"Some fine ass hooligan put that dent there earlier this morning."

She bust out laughing. "Not a hooligan. What you do or better yet didn't do?"

"Oh, it had nothing to do with me. He threw someone up against it," I said, casually. "We had a few words, and he gave me a couple dollars to cover the damage."

"A generous hooligan, I see." She nodded. "I like it."

"Alright, y'all ready?" Brae'lynn returned to the livingroom, refreshed.

"Yeah. I just gotta put my boots on." The metallic boots I'd decided on was another one of those, *Tik Tok made me buy it* purchases that I got from Amazon. Sliding them on my feet, I did a quick run in place to check for comfortability.

"Not us in each other's closet," Asani let out and for the first time since they'd walked in, I got a good look at their outfits. We all had on graphic tees, shorts, and high heeled boots.

"Just the ghetto three stooges," I laughed. "Let's go. I have a feeling that this night is gonna be interesting."

———

ENTERING THE SPORTS BAR, I HAD TO DO A DOUBLE TAKE. THE PLACE was nothing like I'd envisioned. It didn't reek of smoke, and instead of the walls being lined with a bunch of unnecessary sports memorabilia, there were pictures of black sports figures. It was tasteful and not childish. The décor conveyed the owner's goal to be different and I appreciated that. The girls clearly shared my sentiment because we made eye contact and nodded our approval.

"You actually came out." We turned to find a guy standing behind us with a charming smile. His eyes lingered on Brae'lynn longer than the quick glimpse he'd given me and Asani. He was very tall and decent looking, nothing to write home about. He was definitely Brae'lynn's type.

"I said I would," she responded, matching his smile, and leaning into a hug. "I pride myself on keeping my word. These are my best friends, Charisma, and Asani." She pointed to each of us as she made the introduction. "Ladies, this is Prince."

I gave a friendly wave and turned back to the crowd. Brae'lynn chatted it up with dude for a little bit while me and Asani entertained each other with our own conversation. I bobbed my head to the music and sang the lyrics to a few songs. The DJ was on point and I was ready to make my way to the bar for a drink. I hadn't come out to stand next to the entrance the whole night.

I wouldn't dare move without Brae'lynn, though. We moved as a unit when we went out. That included trips to the bar, the bathroom, and most importantly, when it was time to leave, we left together. NO BAD BITCH LEFT BEHIND was my motto.

"Ahem," Asani cleared her throat to get Brae'lynn's attention.

Brae'lynn said something to dude, he pecked her cheek and walked off. "What?" She said, focusing back on me and Asani.

"Nothing. It looked like you were about to be boo'd up and I didn't come out for all that," I made clear.

"Boo'd up with who, Prince? Girl, he cool and be on me, but I'm not interested. Don't mean I don't flirt here and there. It's all in fun."

"Uh, huh. Let's go to the bar and get a drink," I suggested.

"Yes, let's do that. The guy hosting the party paid for an open bar so all the bad bitches can drink for free." With her hands in the air, Brae'lynn escorted us through the crowd and to the bar.

It seemed like we walked through a sea of people to get there. The crowd was cool, though. Everyone was enjoying themselves and I didn't catch any female with the screw face; that was a relief. I hated to come out and have to deal with hating ass bitches who wanted to have a stare off instead of having a good time. The same went for the guys.

"Hello, can I have three Casamigos Reposado with pineapple juice, please?" Asani ordered for each of us.

"How you know I don't want a Hennessy and Coke?" I said with a smirk on my face.

"You came to fight or sip and be cute?" She countered and I winked at her. "Exactly. And I know you don't drink that shit."

Sho'nuff, shorty, what it do? The intro to Usher's "Bad Girl" filled the bar and I threw my hands in the air once the beat dropped. The song screamed main character and it's exactly who I was whenever I heard it. I'd always felt like Usher had made the song specifically for me. I rocked my hips to the beat and as always, Asani pulled her phone out to record, while Brae'lynn shouted, *fuck it up best friend!*

By the time the song had reached the bridge, I'd drawn a crowd. I got to moving like I was the leading lady in one of Usher's performances, further reminding myself that I belonged in Vegas, on stage with him. The song ended and the DJ shouted out, *shorty with the metallic boots, you did that shit!* Making me die laughing.

"Now, that's how you show a motherfucka you outside, bitch!" Brae'lynn boasted while handing me my drink.

I sipped the drink and was pleased with the mix. It wasn't too strong but nowhere near weak. "This is good. We gon' man the bar or find somewhere to sit?" I sipped my drink again and scanned the room for a table.

"Prince said he held us a table next to his. Come on, it's near the back."

"Uhhh, no. I'm not sitting in the back of no establishment that I'm not familiar with, girl. If we can't find a table close to the exit, then I'm good right here."

"Well, cheers to manning the bar," Asani let out, jokingly, toasting her drink in the air. I shrugged my shoulders and hopped up on the available bar stool while Brae'lynn shook her head.

For a minute I thought I was sipping my drink like a lady, but the ice clinking against the glass said otherwise. The drink was too good and I wanted another one. At the far end of the bar, I could see the bartender entertaining a woman. There was no way I was about to yell out to him, so I raised my hand in the air to get his attention instead.

"The bartender's name is Carter, 2A." I turned to the voice and found myself staring into the dark brown irises of Babyface. I could've sworn I felt my heart do a somersault. "You gon' call him or you want me to call him for you?"

"I got this drink just fine before you got here, sir." Turning back around, I put my hand up for the bartender again. Had the girls not been a few feet away having a dance battle, I would've had Brae'lynn's big mouth self get the man's attention. "Excuse me," I called out, only for the bartender to give me the *wait a minute* finger.

"Ayo, Carter!" Babyface yelled out and the bartender's head shot up. Clearly recognizing Babyface, he abruptly ended his conversation and came right over. "The lady wants to order." Babyface nodded towards me and I rolled my eyes.

"Sorry bout that. What can I get you, beautiful?"

"This Reposado and pineapple juice is cool. Thank you."

"And let me get a bottle of water," Babyface ordered.

He took my empty glass and I watched to make sure he wasn't about to reuse it. Seeing him grab another glass from under the bar top, I turned back to Babyface. "I guess I should be thanking you, too, huh?"

"I mean shit, it would show that you grew up with some manners. Don't really make no difference to me, I'm getting my water."

"Not you speaking on manners after this morning."

He smirked at me and I couldn't stop my mouth from doing the same. "I said sorry, shorty. Did your landlord give you any problems?"

"Not yet, but I'm sure it's coming." The bartender sat my drink in front of me and slid the bottle of water over to Babyface. I waited until he walked away then continued talking. "I'm sure I'll see him sometime this weekend. And if he gives me any problems, I'm gon' give you some."

He chuckled lightly. "You tryna box wit' a nigga or sum'n, 2A?"

"Excuse me, we're sorry to interrupt." Brae'lynn could be heard from behind me as she loosely wrapped her arm around my neck. Asani stood on the side of me. "And who might this handsome gentleman be?"

"Babyface?" Asani questioned and I nodded.

"Who the hell is Babyface?" He questioned, the smirk he had was now replaced with a frown.

I giggled and sipped my drink. "What? You been calling me 2A, so I gave you a nickname, too. Yours fits you well."

"Maann, go head, shorty, ain't nothing baby bout me. Excuse me for a minute, though, 2A." Picking up his water bottle, he got up and disappeared in the crowd.

"Well, Babyface is just as fine as he wanna be, huh?" Asani commented.

"Damn sure is," Brae'lynn agreed. "And clearly our friend thinks the same cause she still looking out into the crowd for him."

"Shut up." I laughed and turned on the barstool once she released me. "Ain't nobody thinkin' bout—." My sentence was cut off by a woman's screams. I immediately jumped up, alert.

"Oh, shit," Asani gasped and I followed her eyes to find a man a few feet away, stumbling through the now parted crowd, holding his neck.

"Oh, hell no, come on." I looped Asani's arm in mine since she was closer and pulled Brae'lynn with my free hand.

Rushing us through the moving crowd, I was able to get a glimpse of the man before he fell to the ground, blood pouring from his neck and mouth. Shocked and scared, I didn't stop dragging them until we made it outside to the car.

"Gimmie your keys, Brae'lynn." Noticing how fidgety she was and taking note of the people running out of the bar, I wanted to be out of the vicinity immediately. "Brae'lynn!" I yelled out, "keys." She tossed them to me and we all got in and peeled off. I knew the night would be interesting but had no clue it would turn from sugar to shit so fast.

CHAPTER FOUR – HASAN

I woke up early to a text message from Unc on my burner phone.

Unc: When you take care of business, business will take care of you.

With the text there was two screenshots. One was of my daughter's trust fund and the other was of an account I had in my mother's name. Both had two hefty deposits. I gave both pics a thumbs up before deleting the messages. Sliding the burner phone onto my dresser, I picked up my iPhone that I used for day to day.

I had a missed call and text message from Heather. Swiping her text off the screen, I unlocked the phone to call her. The phone rang once before she answered. I heard my baby crying in the background and my ears perked up.

"Ay, what you got going on over there? Why my baby crying?"

"She's crying because I won't give her the remote," Heather answered.

"Why she can't have it?" I was big on giving my baby whatever she wanted if it made her happy. If that meant I was spoiling her, so be it.

Heather sucked her teeth. **"Well, the first obvious answer would be because I said no. Second, if I give her this remote, I may not ever see it again."**

"Girl, I'll buy you two, just give my baby that one." Bella's crying had ceased and turned into laughs which made me smile. **"Pre-ciate you."**

"Boy, I didn't give her the remote. I gave her her iPad."

I shrugged my shoulders as if she could see me. **"Hey, it did the trick. You called though, wassup?"**

"I keep telling you, you gotta stop letting her do what she wanna do."

"And I keep telling you to stop telling me what to do when it comes to my baby. What you need?" Standing up from my bed, I put the phone on speaker so I could handle my morning hygiene.

"Oh, yeah. I need to take my car to get serviced and I really don't wanna sit in there with Bella because I don't know how long I'll be there. You know she gets real antsy. You think you can meet me over at the Lexus dealership in Westchester for twelve o' clock? If it's an inconvenience, just let me know and I can see if my sister can watch her until you pick her up later."

"That's what she got a father for, Heather. It ain't never an inconvenience when it comes to my baby. Let me hop in the shower and I'll meet you there."

"Send me a pic of that dick when you get out the shower," she whispered into the phone.

"No," I whispered back and laughed.

"Whatever," she replied, sounding salty. **"You've seen one, you've seen 'em all."**

"If that's your way of trying to make yourself feel better about rejection, cool."

"Anyway, thanks for getting her."

"Ain't no thang. Put me on speakerphone real quick so I can talk to my chunk butt."

"I have you on speaker."

"Bells," I called her by her nickname.

"Dada," she responded, followed by a fit of laughter.

"I love you, stinka butt. What you doing?"

"Luhhhh you," was her response and I felt all gushy inside.

"No, Bella, don't throw it, mama." One thing about Bells, she was going to show out with Heather, especially when I was on the phone. **"We'll see you in a few."**

"Aight." I hung up before she could say she loved me. For some reason, Heather thought that if she kept expressing her love for me, it would prompt me to respond the same way. It never did and today wouldn't be any different.

I had let Unc know last night that I was on Bella's time this weekend and that I'd be back on call Monday. It was important for me to spend time with my lil' one and watch her discover new things. Me picking her up earlier than the agreed time was nothing. Shit, in some ways, being around Bella made me feel like I wasn't as heartless as I had to be when I was in the field. It was crazy how a two-year-old could do that.

After a fifteen-minute shower, I washed and moisturized my face, put on a pair of sweatpants, and a white tee. Putting on my watch and chain, I pulled out a fresh pair of Uptowns from the top of my closet, along with a pair of Nike socks. Fully dressed, I looked at myself in the mirror and the name *Babyface* popped into my head. Shorty from Jay's building was wild for referring to me as such. *2A* fit her because of her apartment number. She had taken that and ran with the bogus ass nickname she'd given me.

Unc's sports bar was the last place I expected to run into her again. Shorty was looking right in her short shorts, thighs all meaty and shit. I didn't think she would recognize me but she did. And although our conversation was limited due to the business I had to handle, the banter was cool. She had a slick mouthpiece on her and I fucked with that. So much so, that I was actually looking forward to her landlord giving her the blues so she could come and find a nigga.

Not that I was looking for a girl or anything, but company from a fine ass woman was right up my alley. Grabbing my car keys, phones, and wallet, I headed out of my three-bedroom condo in Jersey. My phone rang as I stepped into the hallway and locked my door. My mother's name flash on the screen. Sliding the green phone button across the screen to answer, the call connected.

"Wassup, ma?"

"Hey, I didn't think you would answer," she spoke with hesitance in her tone.

"Why wouldn't I answer? We beefing or something? If so, you gotta let me know these things. I be having a lot going on."

"No, we're not beefing as you say. It's just you're always on the go, so we barely speak. And what kind of mother beefs with her child?"

I could've responded with, *what kind of mother leaves their child for someone else to raise,* but I let her make it. **"And you barely call, but here we are now. Wassup, though, everything alright with you?"** I hopped in my car, connected the call to my Bluetooth, and drove out of the building's garage.

She went silent for a few moments, likely trying to come up with a response to my comment, but she and I both knew that what I said was a fact.

She cleared her throat instead. **"Yes, I'm fine. If you're not busy Sunday, I want you to stop by for brunch."**

"Uhhh, yeah, I guess I can do that. Bells will be with me, too."

"Even better. Is there any breakfast food she doesn't eat?"

"Eggs," I replied and laughed, thinking about the last time I'd tried to feed eggs to Bells by mixing them in her grits. She'd swiped her plate on the floor and rested her head on her small hand like she was telling me I wasn't slick.

"You gotta put them in the grits like I used to do with you, remember?"

"Yeah, she ain't with it, ma."

"Well, alright, if my grandbaby don't like eggs then I'll take them off the menu."

"Preciate you."

"Umm, I'm only accommodating her." She laughed lightly.

"That's cool. Whatever makes my baby happy makes me happy."

"You're a good dad, Hasan. How you feel about Bella is the same way your dad felt about you at that age. I won't hold you much longer, though. I'll see y'all on Sunday."

"Alright. Have a good day."

"You too, son. I love you."

"You, too," I responded and the call ended. I loved my mother but had a hard time saying the words over the last few years. I knew it'd eventually come naturally to me as it had before she left, but there was some shit I had to heal within myself before I could openly express those words to her again.

———

"Welcome to Lexus of Westchester, my name is..."

"2A," I cut her off before she could look up and finish talking.

"You stalking me now?" She smiled and I chuckled.

Before I could respond, I heard Heather call out for me. "Over here, Has." Turning in her direction, I could see her sitting in what I assumed was the waiting area. Bella was in her lap, likely sleep.

"Nah, I ain't stalking you, shorty. It was good seeing you, though."

"Hey, last night—."

"Charisma, can you come to my office really quick?" A woman called out to her, cutting her off. I was glad she did, cause I didn't know what she was about to ask me.

"Yeah, sure," she responded, glancing behind her. "Good to see you, too, Has." She winked and went about her way.

I watched her briefly, admiring the way her ass naturally jiggled in her maxi skirt as she walked off. Remembering Heather was likely burning a hole in my head, I turned and made my way over to her. "She sleep?" I asked, reaching for Bella.

"Yeah. She's been sleep a few minutes. Do you know that girl at the front?" She questioned, being nosey.

"Nah, not like that. Why?" Bella stirred in my arms and her eyes popped open. "Hey, pretty girl." She smiled up at me and got comfortable in my arms. I kissed the top of her head and squeezed her a little.

"Oh, nothing," Heather responded. "I was tryna see if you had some pull and could cut my wait time in half or better yet, get me a discount on my maintenance." She giggled and I called bullshit but didn't put her on the spot.

"Yeah, sorry, no pull here. If you need help covering the maintenance, you know I got you. That's my baby's means of transportation so you know I gotta make sure she safe. Ain't that right, Bells?" I looked down at Bella who had closed her eyes again.

"Well, shit, is my safety important to you, too?"

"Of course, it is, you're my daughter's mother. I'ma get gone with my baby, though. Have a good day."

"Wait. Let me give her a kiss." She wrapped her arm around me and leaned in to kiss Bella on her cheek.

"Maaann, you a trip," I snickered. "We'll see you on Monday."

"What?" She faked innocence. I didn't feed into it, instead, I reiterated that we'd see her in a couple days.

Walking back to the exit, I spotted who I now knew as Charisma coming my way. I wanted to say something else to her but wanted to avoid Heather doing some weird shit that would have the both of us looking crazy. Instead, I gave her the signature move that was universal amongst the Black community, a head nod. She picked up on it and communicated the same. I had a feeling that I'd be running into Ms. Charisma again. If I was being honest with myself, I hoped the interaction lasted longer than a few minutes.

CHAPTER FIVE – CHARISMA

Now, what were the odds that I would run into this man at the bar last night and now at work this morning? Crazy thing was, today wasn't even my scheduled day to work. Chelsea called me early this morning asking if I could come in to cover the weekend receptionist. I went to say no, knowing I really needed the sleep, but yes came out instead. It was only a 5-hour shift, so I figured I'd knock it out and be home in no time.

For some reason the day had dragged up until Babyface walked in. His face held a pleasant surprise when he entered the dealership and so did mine. Our interaction was brief and just like at the bar, he had to quickly dismiss himself. Only this time he was pulled away by a female. By the way she called out his name, I knew she was in some way staking her claim. I mean, why else would she belt out his name from across the room?

I wanted to ask him about what had occurred at the bar last night and if he'd seen anything. After going over the question in my head and having already pegged him as a street dude, I knew that would've been some police ass shit to ask. So, I dropped it along with any other conversation I may have had for him. Between Ms. Iwannabeseen and Chelsea calling my name, it was clear that there wasn't any time to catch up.

"Hey, Chelsea, what you need?" I asked, entering her office.

"Have you thought about taking the position?"

"You know it's only been 24 hours, right?"

"I knowww," she dragged, "I just really want you to say yes."

I shook my head. "I'll be honest, I'm really leaning on the side of no, Chels. Being in sales isn't my thing. You know what I'm in school for and that already takes a lot out of me. I would be doing myself a disservice if I committed to the position."

She sighed. "I get it. I don't like it, but I get it, and I respect you remaining steadfast when it comes to your goals. I really needed another pitbull on my team."

I smirked at her. "Girl, I ain't no pitbull. You see how cute I am? This is all teacup Yorkie." We both shared a loud laugh.

"Oh, please." She waved me off.

"Now, can I go back out here and finish my shift so I can go home? I had a long night last night."

She smiled. "Yeah, go head and go so I can be sad in peace." She threw her hand up and covered her face.

"Oooh, the drama," I teased and snickered as I left her office.

I'd come out just in time to see Babyface leaving. He had a kid in his arms who appeared to be sleep. Not knowing the deal between him and the female and respecting the boundary, I gave a quick nod as he left out. This being our third run in, I was starting to think that it wasn't a coincidence. Shaking off the thought before it became a thing in my head, I sat down at my desk and went to power on my computer.

"Excuse me, can I ask you something?" I looked up to find the same woman who had called for Babyface's attention standing a few inches from my desk.

"Sure. Is it about your car?" I gave her my undivided attention, already knowing that whatever she was about to ask had nothing to do with her car. Call it women's intuition, or better yet, call it me being able to spot bullshit from a mile away.

"No, that's already being taken care of." I gave her kudos for her honesty. "It's about the guy that just left here."

"Go head." I leaned forward with my hands folded on my desk.

"Do you know him intimately?"

"Girl, what?!" My voice went up two octaves and for a second, I forgot I was at work. "What kind of question is that?" I brought my voice back down but my posture had changed completely.

She shrugged. "This was the best way I could dress up the question, you know, seeing as this is a place of business."

"You know, if you really felt that way, you wouldn't be standing in front of me asking that question. It's not only messy but very tasteless. Not to mention ghetto as hell no matter how much you try to dress it up." I gave her an incredulous look because I couldn't believe the audacity.

"You still haven't answered my question," she pushed with an eye roll.

"And I won't," I said, matter factly.

"Hmph, if that's not a typical response then I don't know what it is. Just an fyi, if you're messing around with him, know that our daughter comes first."

I shook my head at the way this woman was putting on. She was showing her hand and I didn't even know Babyface's real name yet.

"Ma'am," Ross, our service tech, waved to get her attention.

"I think they're ready for you," I advised her, nodding towards Ross. "I also think it's safer over there than over here, if you get my drift." I gave her a fake smile before focusing on my computer.

"Have a good day," she said and walked off, clearly thinking she'd one upped me by making it known that she was the baby mother.

All she did was get her silly ass added to my group chat. *Maannn, me and the girls are gonna have a field day about this one,* I thought to myself as I pulled out my phone and went to our text thread.

Me: Y'all not gon' believe what ghetto ass, "Real House-wives of Atlanta" shit that just happened to me.

———

ONCE THE CLOCK HIT THREE P.M. I WAS CLOCKED OUT AND IN MY car. I hadn't had any further interaction with ol' girl at the dealership but she did give me a dirty look as she left. I paid that shit zero attention because one thing about it, once I took it there, it was no turning back. So, it was best for me to leave well enough alone. Besides, me and the girls had already chewed her up in the group message with gifs and all.

Brae'lynn's response was to get Babyface's number the next time I saw him and mention the incident with his bm. She thought it was best to bring it up then to see his reaction, that way it would determine whether or not I used the number. That shit was out of the question. Me bringing the situation up would mean I was just as pressed as she was. Me finding out the man's full name seemed more important than talking about his child's mother, if I even saw him again.

As I turned onto my street, my phone rung with an incoming call from my mother. I hadn't heard from her the last twenty-four hours and was ready to give her an ear full.

"You know I was about to put an APB out on you, right?" I joked, seriously. We spoke at least once daily so not hearing from her for even a day was an issue.

"Girl, go head, I'm *yo* mama, not the other way around. Why you ain't called me?" My mother was Lisa Raye's doppelganger, from the looks down to her voice. And as she spoke, I could tell she was cutting her eye the same way Lisa Raye did when she was checking someone.

"I'm the child, you supposed to call me, mommy. So, where you been?"

"Where I usually am, girl. At the bakery or in the house. Two places you ain't seen in the last few days, so wassup." My parents owned a bakery on the Eastside of Harlem that they'd operated since I was a little girl.

When my father passed away three years ago, my mother took a step back from the business. In the last year, she'd slowly started to get back in the swing of things and it did my heart good to see her in her element. My father's passing was hard on the both of us, and I still missed him as if he'd just passed yesterday. We both knew that he'd want us to continue living as if he was here, which was why I continued to push through school every day in spite of how I felt.

"I know, mommy. Work and school have consumed me, but

the semester is coming to an end, so I'll have more free time. I went out with Brae'lynn and Asani last night, though." Thinking about how our night ended made me shake my head.

"Okay, okay, did they have to drag you out or did you go without a fight?"

I kissed my teeth. "I'm not that bad, don't do me like that."

"You're right, baby, you're actually *worse*. But, it's all good, how was it?"

Getting out of my car, I hit the locks and walked across the street to my building with the phone to my ear. "I was having a good time up until some mess popped off. We had to clear the scene and quick."

"Just like I taught you. When shit start looking funny, never stand around looking. You get the hell on." She'd been telling me that since I was about eight years old and I'd been moving that way ever since.

We caught up as I entered my building and rode the elevator up to my floor. When the elevator dinged and opened up, the first thing I saw was my landlord, Mr. Baines, examining the dent in my door.

"Mommy, let me call you back. I have something I need to deal with."

"Wait, before you go, I want you to come spend the day with me Sunday. We can go shopping and have brunch."

"Sure, I'm down. And I'll come by the bakery tomorrow to help y'all out."

"Alright, I'm holding you to that."

"I know, which is why I didn't give a time," I replied, laughing.

"You ain't no good. I love you, sugar."

"I love you more, mommy. Talk to you later."

Taking a deep breath, I approached Mr. Baines just as he stood up straight. "How are you, Mr. Baines?"

He turned to me, face already frowned up. "I was doing okay up until I saw this dent in the door. Any idea how it happened and how you plan on fixing it?" He had a rasp to his voice and not a sexy one. He had that rasp that belonged to a chain smoker and a belly that belonged to a beer drinker. It was just big and filled with yeast. That, coupled with his dry face, thin ponytail, and sometimes nasty attitude made me limit my interactions with him.

"Well, first, I don't know how it got there. Secondly, no, I don't plan on fixing it. Excuse me, you're blocking the entrance to my apartment." I gestured with my hand for him to move back and he did.

"I can always run the cameras and see what occurred, Ms. Charisma. And when I do, I'll be taking legal action."

I put one hand on my hip and the other on the door handle. "Oh, please, do me a favor and run them. That way I can see who stole my Amazon package last week. The same package that you have yet to get back to me about." He knew damn well the cameras didn't work and he used them as a scare tactic.

"I am not liable for your personal items being stolen," he argued.

"And I'm not liable for anything that happens outside of my apartment to this building's property, i.e. this door. Now, if you'll excuse me, I'd like to go inside and about my business."

He scoffed, preparing to walk off. "We'll revisit this conversation when it's time to renew your lease."

"That amongst other things. Good day, Mr. Baines." Turning my back to him, I entered my apartment and made sure to slam the door behind me. He had me fucked up thinking he was about to bully me into paying for some shit.

Kicking my shoes off and placing them on the shoe rack, I found myself annoyed with Babyface. If it hadn't been for his overly aggressive ass, I wouldn't even be in this predicament. *Ughh, I wish I had his number so I could call him, curse him out, then hang up on his ass.* I vented out loud to myself but that wasn't enough for me. I needed someone to cosign how I was feeling, so I called Brae'lynn.

"Girl, you gon' live a long time, I was just about to call you." She answered the phone, breathing heavy.

"For what?" My tone had a little stank on it due to my frustration.

"Eww, well, not to tell you I hit the lotto and offer you some of my winnings if that was the case."

A small giggle escaped my lips involuntarily. **"Girl, what?"**

"I'm saying, you sounding all stank, if I was calling with good news, you sure would've put a damper in my mood."

"I'm sorry, I'm just annoyed. I just had words with the landlord about the dent in my door."

"Ohhh, he must've been on some bullshit as always. Did you tell him you had the money to cover the damage?"

"Nope, and I ain't doing shit. He can kiss my ass! I'ma use the money and get me some stuff for the house. Prime day on Amazon coming up anyway. Better yet, I'ma throw it in the stock market. You know I like to see my money make money."

"Right, right. Whoo shit, let me sit down."

"Where you at and what you doing?" I finally got around to asking. Taking a seat on the couch, I tucked my feet under my butt, picked up the remote, and turned on the tv.

"I'm at the gym in my building."

"At the gym?" I questioned, amused. "For what, B?"

"Baby, look, this fine ass man just moved in across the hall from me about two weeks ago and he look like he works out. I've been coming down here every other day fake working out, you know, to see if I run into him. Bitch, why I saw him today and was playing cute like I really wanna be in here? Talkin' bout, I've been looking for a personal trainer and shit. Do you know this nigga took me seriously and was in here tryna kill me? Charisma, it ain't that much dick in the world that would ever make me play myself again. Shit, here he go, hold on."

The phone went silent and I laughed so hard, tears ran down my cheeks. Brae'lynn was a certified nutcase. I waited until she came back on the phone, still cackling because some shit you just couldn't make up. "Hello."

"Girl, yeah. He come over here talkin' bout am I ready to get back at it. Calling a bitch beautiful and shit."

"And what you say you nut?"

"I told him to give me a minute cause I had a family emergency, duh."

"What family emergency, Brae'lynn?" I was too tickled by her antics.

"**You, bitch, duh,**" she chortled. "**No, forreal, on a serious note. I was calling you to tell you that the dude at the bar died, girl.**"

"**Whattt?!**" I shrieked. "**How you know?**"

"**Prince told me. He called to check on us and you know my nosey ass asked what happened. I'm surprised you didn't ask cutie about it when you saw him today.**"

"**I almost did but decided not to at the last minute and I'm glad I did.**"

"**Why, because of the bitch?**"

My face frowned up. "**Hell, no. He just don't seem like the type of person you ask some shit like that.**"

"**Ooohh, I get what you saying.**" She caught my drift without me having to say too much. "**I know what you need to ask him, though.**"

"**And what's that?**" I waited for her to say something slick.

"**What's up with that what's up, ask him what's up with that what's up, what's up!**"

"**Bye, B!**"

She snickered. "**Whatttt? You know Post Malone did his biggest one with that song. And you know you wanna see what's up with cutie. This your third run in with him, you betta let God bless you this Summer.**"

I rolled my eyes. "**That man has a child and a baby mama who's clearly pressed. I'm so good.**"

"**Girl, welcome to 2023, all these niggas got baby mamas that's still pressed. The bitches who ain't be unicorns forreal. Don't let that stop you from what could be. He prolly don't even fuck with her like that.**"

"**Yeah, and he prolly do. I ain't thirsty to find out. Can I go now?**"

"**You called me, heffa, bye!**" She hung up before I could and I giggled. *Babyface being sent for me? Yeah, right,* I thought to myself as I flicked through channels for something to watch.

CHAPTER SIX – HASAN

The weekend had gone by so fast, before I knew it, Sunday was here. Me and my princess tore the streets up the last few days. We went shopping for a bunch of toys and clothes that she didn't need. We hit the movies, Billy Beez, Barnes & Noble, and a kids spa that Liv recommended. Bells loved books so I always made sure that the *Adventures of Daddy and Bella* either started or ended with a trip to Barnes & Noble to add to the little library I had set up in her room. Liv had put me on to something with the spa, too. I was raising a true girly girl and even at two years old, Bells was into getting her nails and toes done.

The whole time we were out, no matter where we were, women flocked to us, openly shooting their shot. Bella wasn't having it. She made sure to cut her eyes at every woman who said she was cute but was fixated on me. The shit was too funny because I knew she was igging the women because she never wanted to share me, but part of me also felt that Heather was teaching her that shit. It was cool, though.

Any bitch throwing pussy while I was with my princess didn't deserve to be around her or me for that matter. Your actions only showed me that at some point you'd be trying to compete with my baby and that was a dead issue.

"Bells, watchu rocking to brunch, princess? I got this short set with the white Uptowns to match daddy or we can do the little dress and sandals." I laid both outfits out with the shoes beside them. I pointed to each fit, waiting for her to decide, only she was too preoccupied with her iPad. "Bells." She looked up with a silly grin before tossing the iPad to the side and standing up in my bed. Doing her best to remain steady, she took steps towards me. Foreseeing a possible tumble, I reached out for her. "Hold on, princess, let daddy help you."

Putting her small hand in mine, we made it to the edge of the bed where the clothes were laid out without incident. She bent down and picked up the dress, holding it close to my face.

"Pwetty, daddy," she squealed, talking as clear as she could.

"Yeah, I like it, too. Come on... let's get you in it so you can make it beautiful, princess." I dressed her in the pink, pleated dress, and pink Gucci gellies to match the pink polish on her toes. I'd showered and got dressed earlier while she busied herself with *Gracie's Corner*, cutting our get ready time significantly. Slicking all of her hair into a curly puff that sat on top of her small head, I lotioned her face real good and put some ChapStick on her lips. It still amazed me how I did this dad shit effortlessly.

"I go, daddy." Bells let me know that I was taking too long by sliding down off my bed and making her way to my partially opened bedroom door.

I laughed. "We going, princess. Let daddy grab your bag and my keys and we outta here." I turned for a quick second and by the time I'd turned back around, she was pulling my door open and scurrying out.

"Daddy, I go," she repeated, taking flight.

Running over to her, I was able to catch her before she could get to the steps. "Got you!" I swooped her up in my arms and tickled her. She giggled, trying to wiggle out of my embrace. "Come on here, Sha'Carri." I jogged down the steps and we took the elevator down to my car.

Ensuring she was secure in her seat, I handed her the iPad and got in the driver seat. As soon as my phone connected to the Bluetooth, it rang.

"**Wassup, Heather,**" I answered and pulled out of the parking garage.

"**Hey, what y'all up to?**"

"**On my way to my mom's crib.**" I checked the rearview mirror to make sure Bella was good.

"**Oh, that's nice. That means you two are in a good place. Good for y'all, Hasan. Didn't I tell you that time would bring the two of you back together.**"

"**Uh, huh. Wassup though, what you need?**" It was only a matter of time before she tried to include herself in the plans and I wanted to avoid that.

"**Rude, are we. And why y'all didn't invite me? You didn't get my message about the picnic?**"

"**Nah, I'm not tryna be rude. You cuttin' into daddy/daughter time, you need something?**" I went around the message about the picnic.

"**No, I was calling to let you know that I spoke to the girl at the dealership.**"

"**What girl at the dealership?**"

She sucked her teeth. "**The one I asked you about.**"

Thinking about 2A, I shook my head. I could always count on Heather to do too fuckin' much. "**And why did you feel the need to do that?**"

"**Ion know, I just did it. I asked her if y'all knew each other intimately. Kinda the same thing I asked you.**" She was so nonchalant about the shit as if it was something that people normally did.

"**That shit was so corny of you, bro. And you know I ain't even out there like that with my business, so even if we were on it like that, she'd know not to confirm or deny shit. Now, you gon' have me out here looking crazy all cause you wanna be messy.**"

"**For somebody who said they didn't know the girl, you sure going real hard.**"

"**And for somebody with a college degree, you sure are missing the point. Heather, let me make this *real* clear to you,** who I stick my **D - I - C - K in,"** I spelled out dick, **"is none of your business. Ion know what you on but don't start with that weird shit. Let me go before you ruin my day."** I was getting tight and teetering on getting disrespectful so I had to cut the conversation short.

"Wait, Has." She stopped me before I could tap the red phone icon on the dashboard. **"I'm sorry I overstepped."**

"No, you not, Heather. You ain't gotta pump fake for me, I know you."

"Whateva, let me speak to my baby."

"Go head, you on speaker." As she spoke to Bella, I tuned her out, thinking about 2A and how she must've been caught off guard when Heather approached her.

"Okay, I'll see y'all on—." I ended the call, cutting her off.

Looking up in the rearview mirror, I spoke to Bells. **"Your mother is a bug out. We gon' make sure that don't rub off on you, okay."**

"Mommy, love," Bella spoke the truth that I already knew.

———

By the time we reached my mom's crib, I'd put the conversation with Heather to the back of my mind. I didn't wanna go into the brunch with a fucked up attitude and ruin it. My mother's house was out in Yonkers. A three bedroom, two bath, with a fenced in backyard that I'd helped her attain through my realtor. Pulling in her driveway, I noticed two cars parked in her garage. One that I knew was hers and the other was a black Lexus Coupe.

She hadn't mentioned having company but then again, I had no way of knowing if the Lexus was hers or not. Getting out of the car, I unstrapped Bells, grabbed her bag, and strolled up to the front door. I could tell the drive had gotten the best of Bells by the way she'd rested her head on my shoulder. This was the time she usually took her nap, so I knew she wouldn't last long. I rang the doorbell and could hear talking on the other side of the door before my mother asked who it was.

"It's Has, ma," I responded.

She opened the door with a big smile and a twinkle in her eye. "You're here."

"You invited me, didn't you?" I returned her smile, letting her know that everything was good. It was crazy that our relationship was so strained that she needed that confirmation. I gave her a half hug and she kissed my cheek while walking around me to see Bella.

"Someone is sleepy, huh."

"Yeah, that drive did it."

"I bet. Is it okay if I lay her down in her room?"

"Her room?" I questioned, confused.

"Yeah. When you helped me get the house, I made sure to set up a room for her. You know, in case you let her come visit by herself one day." Her voice held hope and it did my heart good to know that she thought about Bells.

"Thanks, ma. That's dope and I appreciate it. If you don't mind though, I wanna have her close so I can hear her."

"I get it," she said. "Here, she's sleep already. I'll put her in the livingroom. You'll be able to see her from the dining room and the kitchen." I let her take Bella from me, along with her bag. "I hope you don't mind, I invited a friend and her daughter over."

"Oh, that's the car parked outside?"

"Yeah."

"Aight. I wish you would've told me before hand, but this yo spot, so I ain't trippin'." We fell in step together, with her stopping in the livingroom, and me continuing to the dining room. I stopped mid-step, seeing 2A come out of the kitchen with two glasses in her hand. "2A, ain't no way the world is this small."

Hearing my voice, she paused and pivoted on her heels. Don't ask me why I thought about her on her tippy toes while I dug off in her from the back in that moment, but that's where my mind went.

"Okay, this is starting to get crazy, don't you think?" She switched over to me, moving with confidence. Shorty's walk was mean with her lil' short ass. She didn't switch her hips in an attempt to be sexy either. I could tell that shit was just in her. Stopping in front of me, she cocked her head to the side. "You don't think this is weird?"

"I'd like to think of it as fate," I challenged.

"Hmmm, I don't know about fate. It's actually a little stalkerish." She smirked.

Running my tongue across my teeth, I took a step forward. "Now, how I'm stalking you and this my mama's house?"

"Seriously?" She pressed her lips into a fine line, silently questioning the truth in my statement.

"That's wild. Who goes around claiming somebody as they *mama* and that ain't they mama, shorty?" I could tell she still wasn't convinced. "Ma," I yelled out to my mother.

"Boy, don't yell and she in there sleeping," she lightly scolded me, while walking towards us. "I see you've met, Charisma. This is my son, Hasan. Son, this is my friend Cheryl's daughter."

"I don't know a lot of Cheryl's but the name sounds familiar. Wait, yo momma is Ms. Cheryl, that owns Tastee Bakery on the Eastside in Harlem? The one with all fresh, made to order pastries?" Just thinking about the lemon, poppyseed muffins made my mouth water.

"Yeah, that's the one."

"Word, where is she?" I asked, looking pass Charisma. "And did she bring anything?" Both Charisma and my mother shared a laugh. I smiled a little and then my face dropped, remembering her pops had died a while back. He was a cool old head that used to kick game to me and Boog when we'd stop by the bakery. "I'm sorry about—."

"Ahem," my mother cleared her throat and nudged me.

"It's okay," Charisma assured me through sad eyes.

"Sharon, girl, this is a beautiful house," Ms. Cheryl entered through the back of the house. "Well, if it isn't one of my favorite customers. Where that pretty little girl of yours? Oh, and have you met my pretty girl?" She gave me a hug and I chuckled at the shocked expression on Charisma's face.

"Ma, really?" She griped.

"What?" Ms. Cheryl feigned innocence. "This mine?" She asked, taking one of the drinks from her.

"We've met in passing," I replied, winking at Charisma.

"And my grand is over here in the livingroom sleeping," my mother spoke proudly.

"Aww, okay. Well, let's eat." Ms. Cheryl locked arms with my mother and pulled her along.

"Ay, 2A, when the last time you had a man?"

"Nigga, no, you didn't." She spit out a little of the drink she'd taken a sip of. My hand instinctively went to her chin, wiping the little bit of what slipped out before it could slide down and stain the dress she wore. Her facial expression was a mix between, *nigga did you just touch me* and *damn.*

"My bad, I didn't mean to offend you."

"I'm very offended, but by the way my mother just put me out there, I guess I can't be too mad. And to answer your question, I've been single for a minute."

"Good. That means I ain't gotta be on a nigga's top when I finally start courting you."

"Courting me, huh?"

"Yeah."

"Word to the wise, can't no man court me that got a baby mama out here running wild."

I shook my head as she walked away from me and into the dining room. Heather had already planted seeds before I could plant my own. My baby mama was a hater and that shit was a bad look.

"So, what we eating on?" I asked, entering the dining room and taking a seat across from Charisma and next to my mother.

"I made a little bit of everything. We gonna do this family style. Cheryl, you mind helping me in the kitchen."

The way my mother and Ms. Cheryl were moving, it was obvious that they'd planned this brunch with the goal of hooking their kids up. It was comical and I wasn't even mad.

"I can help, too," Charisma offered.

"We got it," both our mothers responded at the same time and laughed. Once they were out of earshot, I spoke.

"I...." we both went to speak.

"You go first," I suggested.

"I'm sorry. Had I known that this brunch was going to be an episode of *Blind Date,* I would've declined."

"You ain't gotta apologize, 2A. I think it's cute. And besides, I'm the one who needs to be apologizing to you."

"For?"

"My daughter's mother approaching you. She told me about it before I got here."

She raised her glass and tilted it towards me. "Cheers to her for being honest. Tacky as hell for how she carried it but honest nonetheless." She put the glass to her lips and even the way she took a sip was sexy.

"How'd you handle it? Did you tell her I caress your cervix every now and then?"

She gave me a lazy grin. "No, I did not. And even if you were, I still wouldn't have told her. You must be good at that kind of activity though. It's obvious that she wants that old thang back."

"I—."

She put her finger to her lips, cutting me off. "The parents are coming."

I stood to grab the trays from their hands and set the food down on the table. Before digging in, we each took a hand and Ms. Cheryl said grace. During the blessing of the food, I lifted my head and locked eyes with Charisma, with neither one of us looking away until we heard, "Amen." My mind was made up, and I was gonna use this brunch as an opportunity to get to know Charisma and see what she was about. It was clear that the stars were aligned for that purpose alone.

CHAPTER SEVEN – CHARISMA

As I feasted on the spread of grits, sausage, French toast, and assorted fruit, I found myself stealing glances at Hasan. A few times he caught me and would throw a wink my way. I'd playfully roll my eyes and look away. I couldn't believe my mother had set me up. When she called this morning requesting I wear a dress, I should've known something was up. She'd mentioned brunch but neglected to tell me that it was at her friend's house and that we wouldn't be the only people in attendance.

Now, I wasn't surprised that she was trying to fix me up with someone, but the fact that, the someone just so happened to be Babyface was insane. I couldn't get away from this man and not that I was going out of my way to *not* run into him, but us being in the same places at the same time spoke volumes. He seemed to think that it was fate. And now our parents were involved, maybe there was some truth to that. Watching our mothers catch up at the table, completely ignoring us, made me shake my head. I took it as their way of making us talk to each other.

After his apology for his baby mother's delusional antics, I'd made up in my mind that a little conversation wouldn't hurt. And although I'd basically shut down the idea he had of anything more than that, I really didn't mean it. I was putting the ball in his court to see how he'd carry it. I mean, shit, this was the fourth interaction, and if he was serious about courting me, he wouldn't let up.

"How old is your daughter?" I asked, initiating conversation.

He lifted his head from his plate and pointed to himself. "You talking to me?"

I smirked at his pettiness and nodded. "I am."

"Ion wanna talk right now." His response caught me off guard, and my face became flush with embarrassment. "I'm just fuckin' witchu, shorty, lighten up." He reached over the table and touched me for the second time. "Bells is two going on twenty-two. You have any kids?"

Still recovering from his joke, I cleared my throat. "I was about to let you have it if you were serious."

"Why? We been sitting at this table for at least a half hour and you ain't had much of nothing to say to me other than can I pass you a napkin."

He was right, but still, my delivery was different. "I was feeling the situation out. And to answer your question, no, I don't have kids but I do want them. Ideally, I'd like to have four, two girls and two boys. I'm an only child so if I don't make it to four, I at least wanna have two."

He nodded. "Shiddd, the potency on this shit is crazy, you guaranteed a three piece."

I blushed, thinking about how handsome my sons would be. I'd caught a glimpse of his daughter at the dealership and she was pretty, with big, bright eyes. "How you skip courting and slide right into getting me pregnant?"

"Ion know," he shrugged. "I just know based off looks alone, we'd make some beautiful babies. And I thought you didn't let niggas with baby mamas court you. When did the sudden change of heart come about?"

"No, what I said was can't no man with a baby mama running wild court me. But, considering that this is our fourth encounter, I'm willing to throw caution to the wind and get to know you."

The pitter patter of footsteps could be heard on the hardware floors and we all turned our attention to the hallway. We watched his daughter make her way to us in her pretty pink dress and puff on her head, rubbing her little eyes. I couldn't get over how adorable she was.

"Daddy," she called for Babyface who was already up from his seat and halfway to her.

"Right here, Bells," he replied lovingly. Her little legs took flight, running towards him. Watching him embrace her made me feel warm inside.

"He's a catch, ain't he?" my mother whispered. "And he's a great dad, love his little girl." Nodding, I picked up on those attributes.

"I have a highchair for her if you wanna sit her down so she can eat," his mother offered.

"Cool, just show me where it is." Babyface sat back down with his daughter in his lap.

"In the laundry room, still packed in the box," his mother chuckled.

"I don't think she'll be able to wait for the set up," I said, pointing at her picking up a sausage link from Babyface's plate. "Here, pretty." I took a small plate from the stack and put a few links on the plate, cutting them in half.

"Thanks, 2A."

"Why you call her, 2A?" My mother inquired.

"Long story," we said at the same time and laughed.

"Come on, Cheryl, let's go out in the back. I have my record player out there," Babyface's mother excused herself from the table with my mother following behind her, wine glass in hand.

"Could they make it any more obvious that they're tryna get us alone together?"

"Yeah, they pushing hard. Why you think that is?" His question was for me but his focus remained on his daughter, making sure the food made it from her plate into her mouth and not on her dress.

"My mother believes I've passed the timeframe in which a woman should be single. I think she thinks I'm lonely."

"Are you?"

"No, daddy," his daughter let out, shaking her head.

I did the same. "Thank you, boo. Ain't nobody lonely over here."

Babyface laughed. "She ain't agreeing witchu. She just letting me know she don't want any more of her food. Look..." He went to give her another sausage link and she turned her head. "See."

"She's so cute. To directly answer your question though, I'm not lonely. Busy? Yes, but never lonely." Speaking the words out loud, it sounded like I was trying to convince myself more than him.

"Can you see yourself in a relationship? I mean, would you be able to fit a man into your busy schedule?"

"Could you fit a woman into yours?" I countered.

"Who said I had a busy schedule?"

I nodded towards his daughter. "Your schedule is sitting right there on your lap."

"True but answering my question with a question is a sign of avoidance. Gimmie a second to a grab her iPad to keep her occupied." He got up and left the dining room. I took the opportunity to hit the group chat.

Me: Hey whores.

Asani: Hey boo

Brae'lynn: What it do, heffa.

Me: So, my mother is at it again. This whole, come see me so we can hang out was all a ploy to get me to her friend's house so she could play matchmaker.

Asani: 😊 **Aunty Cheryl said she gon' get her a grandbaby by any means necessary.**

Brae'lynn: No, forreal. LOL. Let's get to the real question though, what the man look like? 😊 **Ooh, if he look like he go to the gym, RUN! Them niggas are crazy!**

Me: Lmao, no you're crazy, Brae'lynn. But y'all ain't gon' believe me when I tell you who walked in.

Asani: 👀

Me: BABYFACE

Asani: Quit lyin'!!!!

Brae'lynn: Girlllllll! That is God. If you don't go head and give that man some coochie. The fourth run in, Charisma? Come on, now, that gotta be your soulmate. Fuck him and then ask if he like his clothes washed with the Tide liquid or Gain. Better yet, ask him if his daughter like OMG Dollz or the

Bratz dolls. You bout to be a step mama, you gotta know these things.

Me: I swear I'ma bout to remove you from the group, B. LOL

Brae'lynn: Cause you know I'm speaking the truth, ain't I Sani?

Asani: I gotta agree with Brae'lynn on this one, sis. Things like this don't happen all the time so it's gotta mean something.

Brae'lynn: Boom. And y'all know I tell no lies.

Asani: Just when you had me on your side. Bitch, yes the fuck you do. You just lied right there.

I laughed out loud and let them know that I would catch up with them once I made it back home.

Brae'lynn: Alright, we love you. And on a serious note, get to know him, boo. You gotta look pass the baby mama.

Me: I won't make any promises but I'll be open. And I love y'all too.

Setting my phone down on the table, I waited for Babyface to return. When he didn't after a few minutes, I got up to see what our moms were up to. As I walked to the back of the house, I could hear the two of them talking.

"I'm glad he's coming around now. Have you had the conversation with him yet?" I heard my mother ask.

"Unfortunately, not. We haven't had our one on one yet. He's always moving and...you know I'm still going through my recovery."

"I get it, sis, and I'm so proud of you. Just know that you don't have to go through it alone, Sharon. I'm sure if he knew the reason you had to leave him years ago, he'd understand. Don't let your fear of speaking your truth keep the distance between you and your son."

My mother spoke from a place of compassion and even though I didn't know the full scope of the relationship with Babyface and his mom, my heart went out to the both of them.

"If you go out there, you'll be able to hear better." I spun around quickly, hearing Babyface' voice behind me.

"Shut up," I said. "You think we should clean-up for them? They're having girl talk and I think your mom would appreciate it."

"We can do that. I'll tell you now, we gon' be figuring this shit out together cause I don't know where nothing is in here."

I wanted to ask why that was but surmised that it was way too early for me to touch on that topic. "They say two heads are better than one, let's put that theory to the test." I went to walk off but his daughter held her hand out to me.

"Hand," she let out in her cute, little voice. I didn't react out of respect, instead, I looked at Babyface for direction.

"Ummm."

"You good," he confirmed.

"Hand," the little princess repeated, showing all of her teeth.

"I'd be happy to hold your hand, pretty girl." Finding myself getting misty eyed at the gesture, I blinked a few times to get myself together. *Fate, perhaps?*

———

THE DAY TURNED INTO NIGHT AND BABYFACE, BELLA, AND I found ourselves in his mother's livingroom fully immersed in *Gracie's Corner*, *Coco Melon*, and *Ms. Rachel*. Every time Bella saw something she liked or heard a song she knew, she'd tap her father with excitement. What was even cuter was him singing the songs he knew. We hadn't spoken a word to each other as he was fully in tune with Bella, and I was in awe watching the two of them bond.

"Look at y'all looking like the perfect lil' family." My mother stood at the entryway of the livingroom, watching us with a big, satisfied smile on her face.

"I appreciate y'all cleaning up for me," his mother expressed from behind her.

"No problem," I responded.

"All Charisma's idea," Babyface said, finally using my name.

"You ready to head out, boo?" My mother asked me.

"Uhhhh, yeah," I replied, my voice filled with hesitance. I really wasn't ready to go but didn't want to make it obvious. Somehow, reading my mind, Bella climbed in my lap and laid her head on my chest. All eyes were on me to see what my next move would be.

"Come 'ere, Bells." Babyface went to wrap his arms around Bella to pick her up and she shook her head *no.*

"She's okay," I said, letting him know it wasn't a problem.

"You sure?"

I nodded. "Yes, I'm sure."

"I can take her home later if you're ready to go now, Ms. Cheryl."

"That won't be necessary," I spoke up. "I drove. Pretty girl look like she sleepy anyway. I'll rock her till she falls asleep then we can head out, ma."

"Or," Sharon interjected, "seeing as we all had a drink, or four," she nodded towards my mother, "I'd be happy to host everyone overnight."

"Well, that settles it. And you know I'm not a fan of driving late. We can stay and leave first thing in the morning, that cool with you?" On to what my mother was trying to do, I agreed.

By now, Bella had snuggled up to me, so I wasn't trippin'. Our parents went their way, leaving us alone again for the third time.

"This shit is wild," Babyface let out, followed by a light chuckle.

"That it is," I agreed, assuming he was referring to how tonight's events had unfolded. I held Bella closer to me and kissed her forehead. "Shit, I'm sorry," I apologized, quickly remembering I was no kin to this child who had a mother. And I knew for sure if she was carrying on about her baby father the way she had, she would nut the fuck up behind some random woman kissing her child. "Here, I'll lay her down." Standing up slowly to avoid waking her, I laid her down in between the two of us but closer to him. "I'm so sorry, that was out of pocket."

"I ain't trippin', Charisma. Only three types of people would kiss a child that ain't theirs. A pervert, someone with mental issues, or someone who genuinely has a heart for kids and may have suffered the recent loss of one. Is it kinda weird? Yes, but if I thought you were a pervert or had a mental defect, I wouldn't have let you get near my child."

I didn't know how to respond. There was no justifying kissing this man's daughter on the damn head. Sensing my embarrassment, he reached over and touched my shoulder. My body did something, something I wasn't familiar with, but at the same time, a feeling I wanted to last a bit longer.

"You good, shorty, I promise." I nodded at his reassurance and to my internal dismay, he moved his hand. "Don't go mute on me now. With Bella sleep, we can have an adult conversation."

"And what do you consider an adult conversation, Babyface?" I inquired, all ears.

"The kind where I don't have to spell out certain words because there's listening ears that act as a tape recorder." He pointed to Bella and I giggled at how well she articulated for a two-year-old and paid attention. "And how long are you gonna call me Babyface?"

"I'm not sure. Why, you don't like the nickname?"

"Are you okay with me calling you, 2A?"

"Are you answering my question with a question?" I countered, throwing his shit back at him.

"Touché shorty, touché."

"Mmmhmm." We both went silent, sorting through our thoughts and possibly what to say next. "What do you do for a living?"

"I'm in the field, 2A." He didn't have to elaborate for me to understand and I liked that he didn't lie but didn't fully expose his hand either. "How you feel about that?"

"Why would I have an opinion, let alone a feeling about what you do? We're not dating or in a relationship."

"Yet." He gave me that smirk and I shook my head. "The stars are aligned, Charisma, now all we gotta do is our part. Whatever that may look like."

I had no clue what his crypted message meant, but for once when it came to the opposite sex, I was gonna go with the flow.

CHAPTER EIGHT – HASAN

The ringing of my phone woke me from a peaceful sleep and a lust filled dream that featured Charisma in a few uncompromising positions. I opened my eyes to find her and Bella still fast asleep. Bella had made her way back over to Charisma's lap at some point during the night and it was evident that there was something about her that made Bella feel comfortable. That said a lot because it usually took a minute for Bells to warm up to new people. The phone stopped ringing then started back up almost immediately.

Fishing for it, I found it on the side of the couch. The screen read 8:05a.m. along with an incoming Facetime from Heather. I ignored the Facetime and called her on audio. The phone didn't complete the first full ring before she answered.

"Hey, good morning. I was tryna Facetime you so I could see Bells. Is she up? I don't hear her or *Gracie's Corner.*"

"Nah, she's still sleeping," I said through a yawn. Standing up to use the bathroom, the lingering smell of the Chinese takeout we'd ordered last night was still in the air.

I smiled to myself thinking about the conversation me and Charisma had about our signs over shrimp lo mein and chicken wings. She was into that whole astrology shit. We went back and forth about how bogus I thought that shit was and how women used it against men all the time. Ultimately, the back and forth ended with us agreeing to disagree on some adult shit.

"Hey, did you hear me?" Heather questioned, reminding me she was still on the phone.

"Nah, what you say?" Making it to the bathroom, I sat the phone down on the counter sink and commenced to draining the main vein.

"What you doing?" She probed.

"Taking a leak, Heather, damn." I hit the mute button on the phone and shook my head.

"I was just asking you a question, Has. No need for you to be all uptight early in the morning."

"Oh, shoot, I'm sorry." I heard the bathroom door open, followed by Charisma's apology.

She closed the door just as quick as she opened it and I laughed, giving my dick a few shakes before tucking it away. That was embarrassing moment number four for her. Shorty was on a roll. Pulling up my pants, I washed my hands and peeked over at my phone screen to see that the call was still going. It was a good thing I'd muted the line, cause if I hadn't and she heard Charisma, she'd be ready to use voice recognition to determine who was talking.

"Hello," I spoke, taking her off mute.

"Yeah, I'm here."

"I know, but like I said, Bells is sleep. We'll be headed your way sometime this afternoon."

"Sounds good. How'd the brunch go? Was your mom excited to see Bella and did she eat good? You know your daughter is picky as hell"

"It went well, my mother was happy to see her. Check it though, I'ma bout to go lay back down." I wanted her to get the hint that I didn't wanna talk and give her the opportunity to hang up before I did.

"Oook, well, I'm up. You can give me a call when y'all on the way."

"Got you."

"Alright, lata." She held the line like she was waiting for me to hang up first, so I did.

Returning back to the livingroom, Charisma was up on the couch in her phone, and Bella was back in her original spot. That let me know what happened last night was still bothering her. I'll admit the gesture caught me off guard too, but not in the way she thought. It was clear that she was caught in the moment. Now, had she kissed Bella's head and went on about chilling like it was nothing then I would've thought her ass was crazy.

"Did you need to use the bathroom or you were tryna see what a nigga had going on?"

"Boy, nobody tryna see what you got going on. I found the other bathroom. Sorry for barging in like that. The door was cracked and I didn't hear you at first. I had to pee really bad, too."

"You gon' get tired of apologizing to me, 2A," I joked, wanting her to stop being so tense.

"I already am," she chuckled. "I don't know what's going on with me. First, I kiss your baby, now this. I know I'm giving straight jacket vibes."

"Nah, you not. Maybe it's that retrograde shit people be talkin' bout."

"Yes!" She pointed at me, all dramatic. "Let's blame it on that and pretend that what happened didn't happen."

I stroked my goatee and nodded. "I'll agree to that under one condition."

"Ahh, hell, what is it?"

"Chill out, ain't nothing crazy."

"Okay, tell me." She pushed.

"Let me take you out to dinner again, later tonight." I hadn't taken a female out since Heather.

"Again?" She questioned; brows raised. "When did I miss the first dinner?"

"Yeah. That Chinese food last night and conversation, you wouldn't count that as a first date?"

She laughed. "Negro please. No, that was not a first date."

"Shit, tell me how it's done then, 2A. I ain't been on a date in a while. Plus, you kinda owe me, you know, since you did kiss my baby on the head and shit."

"You know what, you ain't even have to go there. I said I was sorry." She covered her face and I laughed.

I leaned over and moved her hands. "I had to get that one off, shorty. You good, real shit. That's the Old Testament."

"Uh huh. Anyway, I accept your dinner invite. I like to eat, so why not surf and turf on your dime." She stuck her tongue out at me and my dick jumped.

I changed the subject quick before I said some wild shit. "I can tell you like to eat by the way you tore them grits up yesterday."

"Omg, they were so good. All I needed was some scrambled eggs with cheese to mix with it. Bomb!"

"You mix your eggs with your grits?" I inquired, feeling some shit in my chest.

"Yep. It's the only way I'll eat eggs if they're on the same plate."

"Bet." I mentally took note of another box she checked without trying to.

"Can I ask you a question?"

"You just did, but you're welcome to ask another."

She rolled her eyes. "You're full of slick responses, huh."

"That's something we have in common but go head."

"How do you manage dating or even getting to know someone when you have a child and a baby mother whose super invested in who you spend your time with?"

"That's not a hard question to answer. It's not hard to manage. I don't date and haven't been in a committed relationship since being with Bella's mother. Everything has pretty much been casual with me. And after my princess made her debut, and the relationship didn't work out with her mother, I became more selective about who I chose to spend my time with."

She shifted her body, placing her head on one of the throw pillows. "You think not having had a serious relationship since your baby mother may have contributed to her behavior?"

My face twisted up. "Hell, nah. Heather is a grown ass woman. Any decisions I make in my personal life that don't directly affect our child shouldn't even concern her."

"I mean, in theory it shouldn't, but it's clear that it does. I just had a run in with her, remember."

I considered what she said and reasoned that she had a point. "I see where you're coming from, but I can assure you that you won't have that kind of run in again. We co-parent the best way we know how for the sake of our daughter. I don't chill over her house and I don't let her dangle my kid over my head as a way to keep me around. You have nothing to worry about."

"Worried?" She scoffed. "Babyface, with all due respect, I will beat your baby mother thee fuck up. You only get one chance to play with me and she had hers at the dealership. So," she sat up and leaned in, "are you sure you wanna take me out to dinner?"

"Surer now than I was when I first asked a minute ago." She tried to hold back her smile but failed. "This the part where you give me your number, 2A."

"Nu uh, this is the part where you ask me for my number, Hasan. I see I gotta teach you how this dating thing works."

"Oh, we dating now?"

"Ughh, you know what I mean."

"Nah, I know what you said. I like the sound of it, too. Can I have your number, Charisma?"

"Yes. Do you mind if I store myself in?"

Taking my phone out of my pocket, I unlocked it and handed it to her. She typed in her digits and called herself. After making sure she locked me in, she handed the phone back to me. I went into the recent calls to see what she saved herself under and smirked. The last call my phone had made was to **FATE.** She didn't know just how true that was.

―――――

"AIGHT, MA, WE'RE GONNA HEAD OUT. I WANNA GET BELLA HOME before her mother get to blowing up my phone for no reason." I wiped

Bella's hands clean of the fruit my mother had given her for breakfast and picked her up from the highchair that I set up.

Charisma and Ms. Cheryl had left a little bit after we finalized our dinner plans, and I chilled for a little longer, to give my mother some time with Bella. While Bella wasn't all over my mother as she had been with Charisma, she was welcoming, allowing my mother to show her around her room. A room that had been decked out in pink and silver with a whole princess theme. One would think that Bella came here on the regular. She had all kinds of toys, stuffed animals, and even a princess canopy bed set up. Bella gave the bed a few good jumps to break it in.

"Aww, okay. You have a few minutes? I wanna talk to you about something before you go." My mother walked out of the kitchen and into the dining room where me and Bells were seated.

"Yeah, sure. Here, Bells." I propped her iPad up and clicked on YouTube. My mother sat across from me and I waited for her to talk.

"I've been trying to find the right time to talk to you but every time I think about bringing it up, the words escape me. Not because I don't know what to say, but because I wanna make sure that my delivery doesn't come off as, *woe is me*. You know what I mean?"

"Honestly, ma, I don't. Just say what you have to say, I'm all ears." I didn't know what I'd walked into but by her body language, I could tell that whatever she was about to say had been plaguing her for some time.

She took a deep breath and began talking again. "When your father was killed, a part of me died and was buried along with him. That very part of me was the part that enabled me to be a good mother to you and the part that made sound decisions when it came to our lives. I began to operate as a shell of my former self and in doing so, I picked up a really bad drinking habit. You wouldn't have noticed it because you spent a lot of time with your Uncle Myles after your dad's passing. I would often drink myself into a deep slumber, only fixing myself up decent enough for when you came back home a few days to be at least half the mother you deserved. Eventually, the drinking got way out of hand to where it was all I cared to do. I knew I needed help and so did your Uncle Myles which is why he suggested I go to rehab. He even offered to pay the expenses. My response to him was to kiss my ass because at the end of the day, I felt it was his fault your father was killed." Tears fell from her eyes but she continued to speak. "And in my feelings, I gave him you to raise. At the time I felt that it was only right for him to take you on because not only was I fucking up, but I felt that he owed it to both me and your father. The day I left you with your uncle, I got in my car and drove to the closest liquor store. I picked up a bottle of Hennessey and tossed it back like that shit was Kool-Aid. In my drunken state, I drove home and crashed into a parked car. After being knocked out, I woke up in the hospital, handcuffed to the bed railing. Them people threw my ass in jail for a whole year. You'd think I would've learned my lesson from there, but I didn't. I didn't like the taste of the jail alcohol so I picked up a new habit, coke. That got me into a lot of shit and then one day, I had a dream and in that dream, your father cussed me out so bad. Told me how much of a shitty person I was for leaving you behind and abandoning my responsibilities. He let me know that if I didn't make shit right that he'd never forgive me. And you know yo dad, even in the afterlife, if he said some shit, he meant it. I called Myles the next morning and told him what I had going on and that as soon as I got out, I wanted to go straight to rehab, and you know what he said? He said, *sis, I got you.* And he didn't lie. He kept his word by not telling you where I was nor my journey back to health. He said it was my story to tell and... here I am, all these years later, sober."

I let everything she told me sink in before responding. "So, you didn't think I'd be able to receive all of this years ago?"

She wiped the tears from her eyes. "No. I always felt that due to our strained relationship, once I came back that you wouldn't even be interested in hearing it."

I shook my head. "I can't even be mad because I don't know what it took for you to tell me today. I am kinda fucked up though, I ain't gon' lie. All of those years of heaviness and disconnect over something I may have been able to help you through, ma. I could've, no, I would've thugged that shit out witchu. You left me to grieve alone at 13. Dad died but I was still here."

"I know, son, I know and I'll live the rest of my life doing my best to make up for the lost time."

I reached for her hand and squeezed it. "I'll never make you do that. We can't rewind the clock but we can do better going forward. I appreciate you for telling me your truth. It gives me a chance to look at things from a whole different perspective. I love you, ma. We gon' be straight."

"I love you, too, son."

"If you really think about it, you've already taken a step to making things right. Her name is Charisma."

She smirked. "I did good, didn't I?"

"If you only knew."

CHAPTER NINE – CHARISMA

WAKING UP THIS MORNING TO FIND BELLA SNUGGLED UP AGAINST me again made me laugh. She slept peacefully, with her arm sprawled across my lap as if to silently let me know that it was where she wanted to be. Peeking over, I noticed Babyface was no longer in the spot he'd fallen asleep in. Sleep had come to me easier than I expected it to, which surprised me. I didn't do sleepovers with men but falling asleep on the couch with Babyface felt natural. Still feeling like I could use a few more zzz's, I went to close my eyes when the sudden need to pee came over me.

Slowly and carefully moving Bella's arm, I laid her back down and rushed to the bathroom that Babyface's mother had shown us during the house tour. Opening the door and finding Babyface standing at the toilet made me turn right back around. The sheer embarrassment that came over my body made me want to run and hide. After a few seconds of cursing myself out, I found the second bathroom to relieve myself. I made it back to the livingroom before he did and wanted to play sleep but decided to stand in my shit. Only, he didn't make me. To ease my mind about what happened, he made a joke and we moved on, agreeing to pay it as retrograde doing its thing.

From the conversation we had until the wee hours in the morning,

I concluded that Babyface was a great father, he was in the streets to a certain degree, his relationship with his daughter's mother was solely co-parenting(or so he says), and he was funny. He had a way with words just like me and he was a charmer for sure. I was looking forward to dinner later.

"So, did you have a good time?" My mother asked once we pulled up to her place. She'd slept most of the ride home and I was consumed with thoughts of Babyface, so I welcomed the silence.

"I did, but, we really need to discuss how this whole thing was put together. You gotta stop putting me out there like that, mommy."

"As much as I wanna argue you down about it, you're right. I just know what love feels like and I want you to experience that, sugar. You have school, work, me, and your friends, but finding love is priceless, Charisma. It's such a beautiful thing and being loved right by someone special is the cherry on top."

Thinking about the relationship my parents had, all I could remember seeing was love between two imperfect people. I was raised in a healthy environment where my father was the leader and my mother thrived in her femininity. I wanted my future relationship to mirror theirs in some respects, at the same time, it had to be on my time.

"And I get that, mommy. I need you to understand that just because I'm taking my time and being selective, it doesn't mean that I'm ruling out love or a relationship for that matter. You know I've always been picky."

"So, what you're trying to say is, *fall back, ma?*"

"Uhhh, more like, you don't have to worry, you'll get your grandbabies soon enough."

She beamed. "I'll take that. I'm thinking sooner than you'd like to admit, considering the way Hasan's daughter was attached to you yesterday. Ain't she so stinkin' cute."

"Omg, too cute. During the night, she crawled up under me again after I laid her down."

"One thing I know is, kids are big on energy."

"Yeah. I hope she's okay sharing her dad tonight, we have a dinner date tonight." I stopped the car in front of her building and turned to her. "You need me to come up with you?"

"Girl, stop tryna treat me like I'm senile, I got me. You go get you," she looked down in my lap then back up at my face, *"literally."*

Catching on to what she was hinting at, I shooed her out of my car. "Go head on and exit the vehicle cause you being fresh." She giggled and got out. "Out of control!" I yelled from my window.

Still laughing, she blew me a kiss. "I love you. Have fun and be safe."

"I will. Send me a text when you make it inside." She nodded and walked into her building. I waited until she turned the corner to the elevators before pulling off.

Selecting a playlist from the many in my music library, I put it on shuffle. The music was interrupted by a text notification. On the dashboard, I could see that the message was from Babyface. I'd saved his number under his real name with a thinking emoji next to it.

Hasan☺: Be ready at eight.

Me: Okay. Is it a casual dinner or formal?

Hasan☺: I want you to be comfortable but sexy. Whatever that means to you, I'm sure you'll be able to put something together.

Me: See you at eight.

The music resumed and I went over the perfect outfit in my head that would make it hard for Hasan to keep his eyes off me.

"WHAT'S CRAZY TO ME IS, HAD WE NOT COME OVER HERE, YOU wouldn't have even told us about the whole dinner or how your night went. Tell us you don't fuck with us, without telling us you don't fuck with us." Brae'lynn talked shit while applying my lashes. She had been letting me have it since her and Asani walked through the door.

"Not too much closer to my damn eye, Brae'lynn. Get whatever you have to get off your chest before you apply another individual." My head was in her lap as she applied each lash to make my eyes pop. The way we were going about the application was unconventional but normal for us.

"Oh, hush, I got this. Come on and put your head back straight." I straightened my head and she continued. "So, did he tell you where dinner was gonna be?"

"Nope, only to be ready by eight. I should've asked him where, right? You know I'm a picky eater so I like to be prepared."

"Oooh, you've been out of the dating pool that long, Charisma?"

"Watchu mean?" I looked up at her with a raised brow and I'm sure I looked crazy with half the lashes done.

"If a man tells you to be ready by a certain time and y'all going out, especially on the first date, all you need to do is be at the door by 7:55p.m. You don't ask where y'all going ahead of time and meeting there is crazy. You know me and Asani gonna check in anyway."

"I don't know him like that, B. And besides, anytime I go out on a first date, I always meet the man at the location. I need to look up the location so that I'm not walking into anything blindly."

"Yeah, I get that, but sometimes, going with the flow is a good thing, too. Everything doesn't have to be so planned out."

"Mmmm, this butter pecan ice cream is to die for," Asani expressed her delight by smacking her lips. She had been in the kitchen on a zoom call when me and Brae'lynn retired to my room for beauty and bullshit.

"I better have another pint in there, greedy."

"You do. This was only half of one. You picked out your clothes yet?"

"Nope, haven't gotten that far. He said the attire was comfortable but sexy so I figured I'd wear a wraparound dress and high heel sandals. It's not too much but still sexy at the same time."

"I like, I like. Where y'all going?"

"B just asked the same thing, I don't know."

"And I think that's a good thing," Brae'lynn chimed in. "She's letting someone else take the lead for a change."

"You want a nigga to thug me so bad," I teased.

"I really do and cutie is just the person for the job, I know he is."

"And how you know that? We only been around the man one time, B," Asani spoke my thoughts.

"It's his mannerisms added to the fact that she..." she pointed down at me, "...actually spent the night with him, although it was very PG-13. She hasn't said one negative thing about him as a person thus far. Yes, we know that he has a baby mother who's a little off, but there hasn't been one bad thing said about *the man*. Also, he just exudes, *that nigga* kinda energy."

Hearing Brae'lynn speak on how Hasan carried himself, made me think about him being the way he was in the street and how much of that life was embedded in him.

"Okay, I'll give you that," Asani agreed. "I picked up on the same things. You nervous?" She asked me, lifting my legs, placing them over hers, and taking a seat on my bed.

"I'm more nervous about her applying these lashes than I am about the date." I peeked up at Brae'lynn who had the tweezers pointed at me.

"You keep it up and I promise you I'll snatch these bitches off," she threatened. "Keep it up."

"Alright, alright," I giggled. "Seriously though, I'm not nervous, Sani. I'm looking forward to the one on one. He said he hasn't been on a date since being with his daughter's mother."

"You believe him?"

"It's really not for me to believe, honestly. I just said 'okay' and went onto the next subject."

"Okay, all done," Brae'lynn announced, nudging me. "Tell me what you think."

"Walked on that," I complimented, loving how natural the lashes appeared to look.

"As per usual, bookie. You know a bitch does her biggie. That man gon' be callin' you sexy all night."

"And I'm gonna answer to it, too. He gotta know that I know, I'ma bad bitch."

"Period," Asani concurred. "Oooh, can we stay while you get ready?"

"Girl, who was leaving?" Brae'lynn answered for me. "This is a moment in time. I'm staying till cutie rings the doorbell. I'm taking pics and all, boo." She made herself comfortable on my bed, grabbing the remote and turning on the tv.

"Am I going on a date or to prom?" I questioned, curious as to why she felt this was a Kodak moment.

"It's not prom, but it is the first date that will be the beginning of your love story. I'm telling you, I have such a good feeling about this. Look..." she pointed to her arm, "I got goosebumps. Yes, I'm taking in every moment."

I didn't want to speak on it but for some reason, I had a good feeling about Hasan as well. My hesitance in solidifying the feeling with words was solely due to me not wanting to jinx it. Lowkey, I wanted the night to be perfect, but in the back of my mind, if things didn't pan out the way I wanted them to, I was willing to accept it and keep it pushing.

————

THE GIRLS AND I LOUNGED AROUND THE HOUSE FOR A FEW HOURS before I'd decided that it was time for me to get ready. I made sure to take a little longer on my routine, making sure that my legs and underarms were void of any hair. Getting dressed with the girls present was definitely more fun than doing it alone. They both did a good job of helping to ease the butterflies that had crept up in my stomach at the last minute. Between Brae'lynn acting out how she thought the dinner would go and Asani throwing out different restaurants we could hit, before we knew it, eight o' clock had come and gone and no Hasan.

"Maybe something happened, check your phone and see if you have a missed call from him," Asani tried reasoning with me while she stood at my window.

"My volume is on, the phone didn't ring, and it's 9:02. I'm about to change my clothes and do some studying. I have my last test of the semester next week." I went to stand up from the couch and Brae'lynn stopped me.

"Okay, yes, an hour is extreme but you know how men are. And something really could've happened like Sani said. Come on, don't be like that."

"I would've been more understanding of that had he sent a text thirty-two minutes ago, B. If I let this shit slide now, he gon' think this is okay to do in the future."

"See, look, you said *the future*," she pointed out, all animated.

"You know what I meant, B. I'm going to change my clothes, y'all can feel free to let yourselves out or shit, stay the night. I ain't got shit to do."

"Ughhh, say something Sani," Brae'lynn whined as I got up and headed to my room.

There was nothing to say. I got stood up by Babyface and it was what it was. I was annoyed but disappointment was what I felt the most. I blamed myself for listening to Brae'lynn with her, *he's your soulmate* bs. And maybe, just a little part of me was still wrapped up in the conversation that I had with my mother about love and being in a relationship. Either way, Babyface had blew it with me. Changing into a pair of comfortable pajamas, I grabbed my MacBook, workbook, a pencil, and a pen and headed back to the livingroom.

"Y'all wanna watch *Love & Hip Hop*? Y'all know I'm good at multitasking and I'm sure you don't wanna watch me study."

"Nope. I'm going home, I got an attitude," Brae'lynn said, standing up from the couch and putting her purse on her shoulder.

I snickered. "Why the hell you have an attitude? I think that right should be reserved to me in this moment."

"Because you throwing in the towel before you really even step into the ring. You don't leave no room for error."

"No, I don't leave a nigga room to think he can play with me. I can't lower the standard for nobody Brae'lynn, not because of what I think it may be."

"Alright, I can't argue witchu about you."

"I'm glad you know, booka. Now, come on and gimmie a kiss goodbye." I set my books down and held my arms out for a hug. I knew my friends wanted the best for me as well as my mother and I loved them for that. "You leaving, too, Sani?"

"Yeah. I have an early day tomorrow. Ughh, I'm so mad." She pouted, walking over to me and Brae'lynn.

"Y'all are a trip. Were y'all trying to marry me off already?"

"At least get you engaged," Sani said with a smirk.

"Awww, I love y'all." We did a group hug that was interrupted by my ringing doorbell. Before I could ask who it was, Brae'lynn had skipped to the door and looked through the peephole. "Who is it?" I asked her. She turned around, grinning like a Cheshire cat and mouthed, *cutie.* I nodded for her to open the door and Sani squeezed me around my neck.

"Give him a chance to explain," she whispered in my ear. Kissing my cheek, she walked over to Brae'lynn who had opened the door and gestured for Babyface to come inside.

"Better late than never, cutie, but I can't save you any other day, okay."

"I appreciate that," he said.

"Text me when y'all get home," I let out.

"K."

The two of them left my apartment and Babyface stood at the door with two bags in his hands, staring at me. The contents of the bag smelled heavenly, but he wouldn't have known I felt that way by the stoic look on my face.

He was dressed in a Black Lacoste polo shirt, black jeans, and a pair of Jordan's. His hair looked freshly twisted and he had a clean edge up. That alone told me that he was dressed up to go out, why he didn't make it on time was something I wanted to hear.

"I know I may be overstepping by popping up at your crib unannounced but I had to apologize in person. I had important business to handle at the last minute and I didn't have my phone on me at the time. I'm sorry for ruining our date."

"Did you think that showing up here unannounced would make the apology more meaningful?"

"Honestly, I'm not sure. I did want you to be able to look in my eyes to see how sincere I was about it. I even stopped by the restaurant I had reservations for and ordered some food to go. If you ain't tryna hear the apology, I get that. Take the food, call your girls back, and y'all enjoy the rest of the evening."

Thinking about the apology and the balls it took for him to show up, not knowing what my reaction would be, I decided I wasn't gonna be a bitch about the situation.

"You can come in and set the food on the table. I'll get us some plates."

"You sure?"

"I'm sure we can eat together. I still haven't decided if we're going to talk over the meal yet."

"Whatever you say, 2A. It's your world," he conceded. I liked the sound of that.

CHAPTER TEN – HASAN

I pulled up in front of Charisma's building with an apology and food to go along with it. It was a shot in the dark, but I was okay with the possible rejection so long as she heard me out. I had every intention of making our first date a memorable one. From the ride to the restaurant to the dining experience. I'd even done my research on the restaurant, looking over the menu and reviews. I was never this meticulous in my planning. For some reason, it was important that everything was perfect for her.

I didn't expect a call from Uncle Myles to throw a wrench in my plans. He'd called me just as I was getting out the shower. There was a deal going down and he needed his left hand with him. I didn't mention the plans I had, my only response was, where was the location of the meet up spot and what time he wanted me there. Once he gave me the information, I hit Boogie and put him up on game. At that point, I could've hit Charisma and let her know what I had going on, but I reasoned that the meeting would be quick as they normally were.

I didn't account for me breaking one nigga's jaw and sending another to the crossroads for trying to make a deal with counterfeit bills. I knew bullshit was amiss when we entered the warehouse and three scrawny looking ass niggas stood in the middle of the room dressed in button ups and slacks. The shit was so unorganized, they had a huddle right in front of us once Unc reconfirmed the price for the work. Unc got a kick out of the whole scene, which was the reason he stuck around to entertain it. I, on the other hand, was annoyed at the fugazy ass "get money niggas."

Unc had always been an equal opportunist and was cool with everybody eating. And seeing that he was the supplier, it kept his bank account full, too. After the two-minute huddle, they opened the briefcase, revealing the fake ass bills that sat inside. Frustrated with my time being wasted, I stalled off, punching the nigga who stood in the middle of the three stooges in his shit. Before the person closest to him could react, two shots from my Ruger hit him in the chest. Boogie popped the third person who tried to make a run for it. He wasn't quick enough to dodge the two bullets to the back.

Shaking his head, Unc popped the leader in the head, handed his gun to Boogie, and apologized for wasting our time. Putting his hands in his slacks, he casually walked out of the warehouse. We went our separate ways and by the time I reached home to change, it was already close to eight. Still, I didn't call. Instead, I changed my clothes, called the restaurant that I'd made reservations with, and placed a takeout order. Had it been any other woman, I would've said "fuck it," but I had a good feeling about Charisma, so I had to see it through.

"Now, tell me why I shouldn't throw this drink in yo bitch ass face." I looked up from the food to Charisma who stood a couple inches away from me with a cup in her hand. I didn't miss the scowl on her face and wondered if she really was about to throw a drink on a nigga. She bust out laughing, turning the cup over, showing me it was empty.

"Maannn, go head, playing and shit. I really thought you had something in that cup."

"No, *you* the one playing, coming over here a whole hour late. I can't believe you."

"I would've deserved that drink on me, huh?"

"You damn right. And I'm tryna hold it down for the sake of wanting to eat that good as food but I got an attitude forreal." She poked out her bottom lip and I wanted to suck on it.

"I know I'm deadass wrong and a nigga really sorry. It ain't much else I can say, 2A."

"I wanna know why you were late." She crossed her arms and leaned to one side.

"I had something I needed to handle and it couldn't wait." Turning back to the food, I opened the bags and placed the containers on the table.

"Why didn't you just reschedule the date then, Hasan?"

"I didn't want to and I wanted to see you again. Come on, you can still be mad at me, but come eat." I waved her over. "I've never been to this place so I had them give me their top five dishes on the menu." Pulling out a chair for her, I waited until she was seated before doing the same.

"It looks good," she complimented.

"Damn, I forgot to ask you if you were allergic to anything."

"I am. I'm allergic to broke niggas and liars. Everything on this table is good, though. You want anything to drink?" The words flowed through her mouth so cooly, I didn't respond immediately. And not because I fell into either category but because her *boldness* turned me on.

"Water is cool."

"Would you have ordered water if we were at the restaurant?"

"Yeah, and prolly some Don Julio, nothing crazy. Why?"

"Since you ruined the chance to take me out, we might as well make the most of this time. Gimmie a second."

"Where you going, shorty? The food gon' get cold."

"No, it's not. I'll be right back and don't start eating without me."

"Aight." Being that I was the reason we were now having dinner at her crib, I let her take the lead.

My phone vibrated in my pocket and I pulled it out to check it. As if she could sense I was in another woman's presence, Heather's name popped up on my screen. Instead of declining the call, I answered. The sooner I found out what she wanted, the sooner I could get her off the phone.

"Wassup, Heather?"

"Hey, you busy?"

"Yeah, I'm out. Wassup?"

"Oh, I just wanted to talk to you about something."

"Does it have anything to do with Bells?" Her silence told me that whatever she had to say next was now going to include Bella to keep me on the phone.

"It kinda does but—."

"Damn," I let out. Charisma had reappeared, dressed up in a pair of heels with a bottle of water, a bottle of Don Julio, and two glasses she was trying to balance.

"A little help here," Charisma requested, pulling me from my internal thoughts of clearing her table of the food and feasting on her instead.

"Wow, you with someone?" The disdain poured out of Heather's mouth so heavy, I felt it through the phone.

"Yeah, lemme go cause I'm being rude right now." I hung up and stood up to help Charisma. "You look good."

"Thank you. I decided not to waste a perfectly good outfit. I ain't gon' lie, I may have to replay it in a month or so since I have no pictures in it."

I chuckled at her seriousness. "That's gangsta."

"What, the fact that I would wear an outfit twice?" She sat down and cracked open the Don.

"No, the fact that you're telling me."

"Oh, shoot, I don't have anything to hide and I'm not one to put on appearances for anyone. What do you want from here?" She pointed to the trays of food.

"Umm, I'ma take the steak bites and the mac. According to one of the employees, the mac is hittin'.'"

"Okay, you pour the drinks and I'll fix our plates. What, why you looking at me like that?" She questioned, putting our plates together.

"Nothing. After showing up late, I half expected you not to even wanna eat."

She shrugged. "Well, good thing for you is that we're getting to know each other. I can't hold anything over your head right now. I did want to be wined and dined and run up a tab. This is nice, too." She handed me my plate and took her drink.

"Thanks for giving me a chance to make it right." I lifted my glass. "Let's make a toast."

She sat and did the same. "To what, you not being late anymore?" She stuck out her tongue and playfully rolled her eyes.

"Nah. Let's toast to fate."

"Hmmm, okay. To fate." Our glasses clinked and, in my head, we sealed the deal.

———

"YO ASS IS DEAD OVER THERE CHEATING, BABYFACE. I CAN'T BELIEVE you," Charisma complained and I enjoyed her pouting.

We were in an intense game of Uno and I had already won four out of the five games we'd played. Currently on our sixth as per her request, I planned on continuing my winning streak.

"How I'm cheatin'? You put down your draw two and I put down my draw four."

"Because Hasan, you gotta draw your cards. That's the rules of the game."

"Not if I got a draw four, shorty." I couldn't stop laughing. "You want me to let you win and that ain't happening."

"You know what…" she smacked down a draw four card of her own on top of mine, "…draw ten, nigga!" Hopping up from the table, she hit the chicken head dance. Moving her body in a circle and twisting her arms.

"Ahhh, I see what you just did there. I'ma pick up the ten, you still gon' lose, though. I ain't even trippin'."

"Well, since you ain't trippin'," she leaned forward on the table, "go head and bet sum'n."

"So, you want me to take yo' money, 2A?" I matched her gaze, loving her energy.

"If you scared, go to church, Babyface."

"Oh, word? If I win this hand, you let me kiss you." My wager made her lips form a straight line. There was no immediate comeback.

"And if I win, you gotta give me all the money in your pockets and a foot massage." She sat back with a satisfied smirk like she'd already won.

I agreed, knowing I only had a few hundred dollars in my pocket. I'd also seen her pretty toes when I came in. "Reverse back to me, skip you, draw four, baby." I threw out card after card and she bit her lip, shifting in her chair. "Wassup, what we doing?" She was down to two cards, thinking hard, contemplating her next move.

"I don't know what you doing, but Uno, Uno out." She put down two draw four cards, stood up, pushed her chair in, and walked around the table to me. Pulling out the chair closest to me, she sat down and put her feet in my lap. "Make sure you give the baby toe extra attention. People always leave the baby toe out."

I laughed. "You mind moving your feet so I can get your money out my pocket?"

"Mmm, I'd much rather have the massage first. I ain't letting you leave without a shakedown anyway." She wiggled her toes and pointed. 'Whenever you're ready, Babyface."

I set the cards down on the table and took a foot in my hand. For a second, she pulled back like she was rethinking her decision. I gave it a small tug followed by a squeeze. She asked for the massage and I was going to make sure I held up my end of the deal.

"Are we gonna talk about the last time you were in a relationship?" I inquired.

"About a year ago." I watched her shoulders relax and eyes close.

"Were you in love?"

"I loved his representative."

"Make that make sense."

"I loved the person he showed me till he could no longer pretend and showed his true colors. Hence, the reason we're not together."

"I respect that."

"Oooh, mmhmm." She moaned as I kneaded the sole of her foot, up to her toes.

"Let me know if I'm hurting you."

"I will," she responded, lightly.

"Did you like the food?"

"Yes. You gotta take me there next time. I'm sure the food is even better when you dine in."

"So, I'm locked in for another date, huh?"

She opened her eyes and nodded. "Yeah. Tonight turned out better than I expected. And to think you were almost put on the *fuck nigga blocklist*."

"Yeah, that's definitely not a place that a man of my caliber should be."

"Where's the humility?" She grinned.

"I left it in my car." We both laughed and I picked up her other foot. "You have pretty feet."

"Thank you. You have nice lips."

"Yeah, I wanna kiss you, too, 2A."

She blushed hard. "That's not what I said."

"I know, but it's what you're implying and I'm with that."

Smiling sheepishly, she replied. "You wanna kiss me, Hasan?"

"I do."

"If I put my lips on yours, you promise not to go tellin' everybody?"

"Girl, you don't know who I know. Bring them sexy ass lips over here." Letting her feet down gently, I pulled her chair towards me until our faces were mere inches from each other.

Our lips were like magnets as they collided. The kiss had come so naturally, before I knew it, my tongue was in her mouth. Things were heating up, and I wasn't gonna be the one to slow it down.

CHAPTER ELEVEN – CHARISMA

THIS FEELING THAT HAD MY KNEES BUCKLING WAS ONE THAT I'D been trying my best to avoid. The feeling that made me moist in the middle, caused the hairs on my neck to stand up, and my knees to buckle. Babyface's kiss was so perfect. Subtle at first, I assumed to gage my reaction, then the kiss deepened, heightening all of my senses. What the fuck was logic at this point? In this moment, me and Babyface weren't strangers who had a few run ins, no, we were two people who felt a connection and were about to act on our curiosities.

As I went to reach for his face, he broke the kiss. His lust filled eyes undressed me silently, and I felt naked under his gaze. Our lips had only been parted for seconds, yet my heart hadn't reached its normal rhythm. My body temperature hadn't come down, and my head was spinning. Even if I wanted to fake like the kiss meant nothing, my body failed me.

"Charisma." He spoke my name in a low tone.

"Yes, Hasan."

"I wanna make you cum. Then, I wanna go to sleep with you nestled in my arms. Tonight, I want you to be *mine*, and if at any point you feel like it's too much, whether in the middle of the night or in the morning, cool. I gotta have you ***now*** though, ma."

I sucked in a deep breath and released it, along with any doubt of this being a bad idea. I wanted to see just how far this *fate* thing could go. If our chemistry in the bedroom was anything like our conversation, then I wouldn't feel bad about giving up the goods so soon. Standing up, I reached out for his hand and put it under my dress for him to feel how wet I was. Clearly used to taking the lead, he grabbed hold of my thigh and gave it a squeeze.

Slowly, he raised my dress up over my waist, giving him an eyeful of my fat pussy. My girl sat up and was so puffy, you couldn't ignore her if you wanted to. Hasan used his index finger to pull my panties to the side, exposing my freshly waxed mound. It glistened under the light in my dining area.

"Hasan," I whispered, only to be silenced by him sliding his finger down my slit before inserting it into my tight hole. "Ooouu... ooouu... yes..." my satisfaction was audible as one finger turned into two. Gripping his shoulders for balance, I rocked back and forth on his fingers.

"Put your leg up here, shorty. Lemme see what this pretty pussy taste like. She smell good."

"Shittt, you gotta move your hand for me to put my leg up, Hasan."

"I know, baby, I'm just locked in on fat ma right now. You hear her talking to me? Shhh, listen." The sounds of my wetness could be heard as he finger fucked me.

"Mmmm, you gonna make me cum. It's been a while Hasan... I swear I'm gonna cum right now." I felt the orgasm mounting.

"You can't cum yet, Charisma. Not yet, baby." Taking his fingers out, he put them to his nose and then stuck them in his mouth. Any other female who had bad hygiene would've taken offense but I knew I smelled fresh.

With all confidence, I put my leg up on his shoulder with a lazy smile. "You better not make me fall."

Ignoring me, in one tug, he ripped my thong off and tossed it to the floor. Gripping my ass cheeks with one hand, he held my leg in place with the other, he flattened his tongue and licked my slit, making my body shiver. I panted, wanting more. Not wanting to rush him, yet still needing the release, I pushed my hips forward. He picked up on it and sucked my clit into his mouth while adding the two fingers back. I was in heaven.

"God, yesss. Shittt... just like that... please don't stop," I cried out. He sped up the finger motion, applying pressure to my g-spot. "I'm cummin'..." I screamed out as my juices poured out of me and into his mouth.

"Mmmhmm, come on, baby, gimmie that good shit." His encouraging words only made me rain more as he held me in place, mouth still attached to me. I was too outdone, dropping my head onto his, trying to catch my breath. "Can I massage your cervix?" He whispered. I had no words, but I nodded my approval. I was his for the taken. "Where's your bedroom?" He asked, lifting me off my feet.

I pointed to the back. "First door on the left." He started in that direction with me in his arms. I took the opportunity to kiss and lick on his neck. Feeling him harden under me, I moved my lips from his neck to his face. Parting his lips with my tongue, I kissed him nastily.

"Damn, you got my dick hard as fuck," he uttered. We made it to my bedroom, where I slid down off of him slowly, making sure that my pussy brushed up against that dick.

Void of words, I pulled my dress over my head, and let it fall to the floor. Climbing onto the bed, I laid on my back and spread my legs so that they were in the shape of a V. Babyface undressed fully and stroked his already hard dick. I salivated at the length and the curve of it. Making his way over to me, he stopped before putting his mushroom shaped head at my opening.

"I'm sure, Hasan." Just as the confirmation left my lips, he entered me. "Sssssss," I hissed at him filling me up to the hilt. He took his time, thrusting in and out of me, making me feel so good. I toyed with my nipples and spread my legs wider, giving him full access.

"Shit, this some good ass pussy. Girl, where you been hiding at? Come here." Leaning forward, he kissed my lips hungrily, strokes still hitting.

"Uhhhh... ooou... harder," I pressed. Giving me what I wanted, he twisted his hips and attacked my g-spot harder. "Ahhhh," I screamed out in pure ecstasy. "Shit, I'm fucking cummin' again!" I fucked him back and he took it as a challenge.

"Yeah, fuck me back." Spitting on my pussy, he massaged his spit into my swollen clit, making circular motions, and right then and there, I knew why his baby mother felt the need to approach me on a whim. Hasan was laying *A1* pipe. "Come on and buss so I can cum witchu." He gave my pussy a light slap, and clit a squeeze. In response, I tightened my walls around him, pulling him in deeper. "Goddamn, you ain't playing fair, ma."

"I'm cummin'!!"

"Shitttt, me too!" He grunted. Before I could tell him to pull out, he'd already painted my insides and collapsed on top of me. "I'm willing to take care of whatever come outta you, 2A," he said in my ear, kissing my neck.

I didn't respond, instead I wrapped my legs around his waist and moved my hips upward, signaling that I was ready for round two.

———

I woke up the next morning feeling weighted down by something. Pulling the sheet back, I found both Babyface's arm and leg wrapped around my body. We were still naked from the night before and he appeared to be comfortable so I left him alone. I'd lowkey been craving this kind of intimacy and Babyface falling right into the way I'd envisioned waking up to a man was too crazy. We'd stayed up all night exploring each other's bodies and by now, I knew that his tongue knew every crevice of mine. The images of different positions he'd put me in flooded my mind, coming back to me in 3D.

"You good?" He asked.

"Mmmhmm, I thought you were still sleeping. You okay?"

"Yeah, I'm straight. Well rested, actually." He kissed the back of my neck and pulled me closer to him. My instinctual response to the hold he had on my body was to kiss his arm that rested underneath my head, but I held off. "I don't know why this feels *natural* to me."

"What, laying in my bed naked?" I joked.

"That and you waking up before me and I'm still here. I put a hurting on that cat, huh?" He squeezed my butt and I hit his arm.

"Shut up. You're still here because I'm comfortable, maybe a little too comfortable, but hey."

"Me, too. Earlier this morning reminded me of just how much of a stranger I really am. I got up to use the bathroom and didn't know where to go. And it was dark as hell."

"Why didn't you wake me up?" I giggled, thinking about him trying to find his way.

"I ain't wanna interrupt your sleep. Besides, had I woke you, I would've had no choice but to put this dick on you again. I used the flashlight on my phone and made it work." I felt his dick poke me and turned around so that we were face to face.

Scooting back a little so that out breaths weren't at war with each other, I admired his facial structure. "What happened here?" I touched the scar underneath his eye.

"Got into a little scuffle on the yard a while ago."

"The yard? You were in prison?" I didn't try to hide the sharpness in my tone due to my shock.

"Nah, girl. I'm talkin' bout the playground in first grade." His face was straight and then he cracked a smile.

"You're annoying." I playfully mushed his head. "Why you ain't just say the playground, Hasan."

"The way I said it makes for a better story. But, yeah, I got into a scuffle that resulted in this. The nigga I beat up got it way worse, though. My pops had me boxing early."

"So, you were a menace in first grade?"

"Shit, I tore pre-k up, too. I eventually got it together in fifth grade. I started to notice that the girls in my school were running from me instead of to me. I changed my ways quick."

"Is that what the girls do now, run to you?"

"Honestly, yeah. But I ain't never been on it like this."

"Like what?" I sat up, using my arm to hold my head up.

"You want an explanation for everything, huh?"

Smiling, I nodded. "Something like that. For every answer, you get a prize."

He looked down at me then back up. His phone rang before he could say whatever nasty thing that was on his mind. Rolling over, he picked it up, silenced it, and put it back down. Turning back to me, he rubbed my thigh.

"A prize, huh?"

"Uh, huh. You can answer your phone. I appreciate you being considerate."

"It wasn't important." The phone rang again and I sat up fully, smirking.

"I think it is. Take your call, I'm gonna go kill this morning breath. I'll be back." Removing the sheet from my body, I stretched.

"How the fuck you make stretching look sexy?"

I turned slightly, winked at him, and got up from the bed. Grabbing my robe from the closet door, I walked out of the room and into the bathroom. Closing the door behind me, I sat down on the toilet for my morning pee. This was where I usually replayed my night or planned my day. This morning, all that consumed my mind was Babyface and where we would go from here. I wasn't looking to jump right into a relationship with him but I did enjoy his company and wouldn't mind spending time like this with him. Finishing up, I washed my hands and continued my morning routine.

After cleansing my face and moisturizing, I took in my new glow. It wasn't the *sleep came easy to me last night* glow, this was that *poundtown, just left poundtown* glow. It looked good on me, too. Feeling fresh, I opened the bathroom door and Hasan stood on the other side of it. He pushed me back until my back was against the sink and held my waist.

"I don't know what you expect after last night, but I know that I wanna have more nights like this where we talk and fuck, fuck some more, talk some more, and you know, shit like that."

I blushed. "You mean, get to know each other?"

"That's what I said."

"No, it's not. I'm in agreeance, though. You know, people call that *dating*."

He bent down and kissed my lips. "I wanna **date** you, then."

"Here's the thing, since we went *raw dawg* last night, and I let you kiss me in the mouth before brushing your teeth, it's only right that we date each other *exclusively*." Removing my robe from my body completely, he sat me up on the sink and slid into me with ease. "Fuuckkk."

"The fact that you even thought this pussy was still yours after I slid up in it, is wild. We exclusive like a muhfucka, 2A." Hasan continued to write his name on my pussy and I let him in celebration of our new dating journey together.

CHAPTER TWELVE – HASAN

Today was my baby's birthday and we had rented out a small party place to celebrate at Heather's request. I didn't mind because my princess had reached another milestone along life's journey and if she wanted to have a party every year, we would. Not only was today special for Bells but Charisma and I had also reached a milestone. We were a month into this exclusive dating thing and going strong. Everything was smooth sailing with Charisma, too.

We made time for each other without having to ask and made sure not to interfere with our daily agendas for ourselves. Charisma had changed my mind and my whole idea of dating. Our dates didn't always consist of us going out, sometimes I would show up to her crib and she would have games set up for a game night. I'm talking Connect four, Monopoly, Checkers, and Backgammon type games. She also liked the relationship cards that helped facilitate conversations about our past and future.

Shit, one day I came over and she talked me into helping her rearrange her whole apartment. While I was tired as hell after, I enjoyed her company, the jokes, and her feeding me during our breaks, both food and pussy.

"Aye, Heather, is somebody over at the venue? I wanna drop

this cake off before I head home to get ready." I spoke to Heather on the phone while securing the cake that Ms. B had baked for Bells in the backseat of my car. Ms. B had surprised me with her skills and saved me some money by making the cake and sending it as one of Bells' birthday presents.

"Yeah, the party planner should be. Do you know what time you'll be there for the party?"

"When it starts. What kinda question is that?" I hopped in the driver's seat and pulled off, careful not to make any sharp turns.

"Oh, I'm just asking because my boyfriend wanted to stop by with a gift for Bella."

I laughed, already seeing what type of time she was on. **"What you want me to say to that, Heather?"**

"I don't follow you," she replied, playing slow.

"I don't care what yo nigga do. But this ain't the event for no meet and greet so you can kill that shit, now. Don't make me get outta my body at my baby's party. Be the fuck cool, dawg."

"Why you getting all hostile? I'm letting you know as a courtesy. I don't say anything about you and yo' little girlfriend."

"That's because you can't. I don't do the shit you do. Let's just have a good day off the strength of our child, aight."

"We will."

"Cool, see you at two."

Knowing the type of stunts Heather liked to pull, I texted my mother to see where she was. I would have her take the cake and keep an eye on everything. She let me know that she was at Ms. Cheryl's bakery, so I made a quick detour there. Since she'd finally been straight up with me about what led her to leaving me with Uncle Myles, our relationship had taken leaps. I called her more and no longer screened her calls. I'd filled Charisma in on our relationship during one of our late-night talks and she commended me for giving my mother the opportunity to make it right.

Arriving at the bakery, I parked out front and spotted Charisma walking out alongside her friend Asani. My baby looked good in a pair of jeans, a wife beater, sneakers, and a fitted cap. What female you know rocking a fitted cap and still making that shit look good? I'd only seen a handful and she was one of them. Her style couldn't be described because she just did her own thing. Whether casual or dressed up, she had it.

"Hey, you," she greeted as I walked around the car and onto the curb. She wrapped her arms around my neck, and I embraced her, making sure to squeeze her tight and give her a wet willy. "Ughh, I hate when you do that, Hasan."

"I know," I chuckled. "Gimmie kiss." I poked my lips out and she kissed them twice. Her breath smelled minty fresh.

"Aww, how cute," Asani said.

"What's going on, Asani?"

"Hey, Hasan, nothing much. Oh, lemme get this, it may be an offer on your space. You better hurry up and decide what you wanna do." She walked off from us, for privacy.

"You heard her, right?" Charisma further pushed.

"Yep. What you up to?"

"Just came by to see if my mom needed help with anything. Your mother's inside."

"I know. I came to see if she could drop this cake off for me."

"Oook. Have you seen the birthday girl yet?"

"Yeah, this morning. I facetimed her to say, 'happy birthday.' She was already up and on 10."

"I bet. The big three is a big deal. I got her something, too. You can come by the house tomorrow to get it if you're not too busy." She kissed my lips again and twirled one of my curls in her hand.

"Why you ain't give it to me last night? I could've given it to her at the party."

"Nah. We're doing so well, I wanna avoid any unnecessary drama."

"I get that, thank you." Another thing I liked about Charisma was that she wasn't problematic at all. And she'd already created a boundary when it came to her interactions with Bella. Since the sleepover at my mom's crib, she hadn't seen Bella in person. They did talk via Facetime whenever she called and I had Bella with me.

"Can you believe it's been a month already?"

I shook my head. "Nah, I thought you would've been tired of a nigga by now. That month went by hella fast."

"Not the least bit tired of you. I wish we could spend more time but as we keep going, I'm sure we'll figure it out."

"All you gotta do is say what you want and I'll move some things around to make it work. What you wanna do to celebrate our one-month anniversary?"

"People don't celebrate one-month, crazy man."

"We ain't people. We Hasan and Charisma and we celebrate round these parts, so what you wanna do?"

"We don't have to. How bout you come over to the house tomorrow and help me study."

"Study? Ain't the semester over? And why you keep saying *tomorrow*? A nigga can't come through later?"

"Of course, you can. I just figured with Bells' birthday, you'd wanna have her overnight. Ooh, wait." She covered her mouth with her hand and pulled away from my embrace quick. Scurrying to the back of my car, she leaned over and threw up.

"The hell? You aight, ma?" I rubbed her back. She spit and nodded.

"Here, boo." I heard Asani say from the side of me. She handed Charisma a few tissues and Charisma stood up straight to wipe her mouth. "Girl, are you okay? That's the second —." Charisma cut her eye at Asani, making her go silent.

"This happened more than once today?" I questioned with a blank stare.

"No, and I'm fine." Wiping her mouth again, she tossed the napkin in the street. "You need to hurry up and get the cake to the party. I'll see you later. I would kiss you but..." she chuckled, nervously.

I kissed her forehead, then her cheek. "Text me when you get home, aight." She nodded. "You gon' make sure she's good, Asani?"

"I sure am," she assured me. They locked arms and walked down the block. Something was off and not in a bad way, but there was defi-nitely *something* that Charisma wasn't telling me. I planned to find out later tonight.

———

HAPPY BIRTHDAY TO YA, HAPPY BIRTHDAY TO YA, HAPPY BIRTHDAYYY. Heather's family and the people closest to me sang out loud while I held Bella with Heather at my side, behind the cake table. *Are ya one, are ya two, are ya three?* Bella clapped at three, making everyone laugh.

Once the birthday song ended, the DJ started back up and I put Bella down to run freely. The party had a good turnout. It was intimate due to my small circle and Heather didn't fuck with too many people.

"Bro, why you let Heather talk you into throwing Bells a mini wedding reception?" Boog joked, headed in my direction with a Capri Sun in his hand.

"You know there's sodas in there, right?"

"Yep, but this strawberry kiwi joint hittin'. What you think about my gift? My niece bout to show up all the kids at the daycare."

"It's fire, just tryna figure out how I'ma fit that shit in my car." Boog had gone out and brought an electric Mercedes Benz ride-on car. It had a pink bow on it and stood out amongst the other gifts on the table.

"Shit, Ion know. I had my girl bring it here in her truck."

"What girl, nigga?"

"You ain't the only one out here hanging up yo' jersey, my boy."

Boogie knew about me and Charisma but I hadn't claimed her as *my girl* out loud, even though that's how I felt. We fit well together so I didn't have to put a title on it, at least I didn't think so.

"Here you go managing to find yo way in my business, dawg. We talkin' bout *you*."

He chuckled and sipped the Capri Sun, looking stupid as hell. "I know. I made it official with my new shorty that I told you about a minute ago."

"Oh, word?"

"Yeah, had to. Shorty is definitely a diamond in the rough. I really like her. She don't take no shit from me either. I think that's what I like the most. Now, don't confuse that with thinking a nigga don't wear the Amiri's around this bitch still. I'm just saying, she don't let me play with her like I used to do these other broads."

I held my hands up. "Hey, I get it. Charisma made me step my shit up, forreal. Like, on a whole other level. Dawg, she surprised me with a showing for a commercial space for the shop. I had only mentioned it to her a week or so prior. Blew my fucking mind." What I thought was an impromptu date night turned out to be a whole property showing with Asani. That shit got Charisma major cool points for even thinking of something so unique and thoughtful.

"That's wassup. Has she had any run-ins with Heather? You know she still psyched out bout you."

"Nah, she hasn't. Not since she pulled that dumb shit at her job. Heather be cool once I call her out on her shit."

"Well, look at us, cuffed up for the Summer. I never thought I'd see the day."

I smiled. "Yeah, me either."

"Daddyyy," Bells called out, running my way. I caught her and swung her in the air.

"Wassup, birthday girl. You ready to open your gifts?"

"We can do that after she takes some pictures," Heather said, walking up. "Every time the camera man is ready, she goes sprinting."

"She's having a good time. Let my baby enjoy her party."

"Aye, I'ma head out. I got some sh—stuff to handle." Boog dapped me up, tickled Bells, and said his goodbyes to Heather before leaving.

My phone rang, and I switched Bells to my other arm so that I could answer it. It was Charisma calling. Stepping away from Heather, I answered the call.

"Wassup, ma, how you feeling?"

"Get down, daddy." Bells did her best to wiggle out of my arms, so I let her and she darted towards her mother.

*"You might as well tell him, Charisma. You can't just not say **nothing**."*

"I just found out my damn self, Brae'lynn, can I take this shit in?"

I overheard Charisma talking on what must've been a butt dial to me.

"You wanna take another one just to be sure?"

*"Asani, don't do that. She done took **three** already, the shit say——."*

Before the sentence could be finished, the call disconnected. Leaving me stuck and wanting answers. The word *test* lingered in my head for the remainder of the party. And while I remained engaged for the sake of my Bella, the phone call was on my mind heavy. Once the party was over, I packed some of the gifts in Heather's car and whatever could fit in mine, while my mother volunteered to take the ride-on in her car.

I strapped a worn-out Bella in her carseat and kissed her forehead before closing the door to Heather's car.

"Hey, can you come here for a second?" Heather spoke from the driver's side window. I walked over and stood in front of it.

"You made sure you got everything?"

"Yeah. I let my sister take home the left-over cake. I figured you probably wouldn't want it."

"That's cool. My baby is pooped, she knocked out back there." Heather glanced back and nodded.

"Would you ever consider getting back together?"

"Are you ready to hear the truth?"

She sighed. "Yeah, Has."

"Well, it's the same as it's been since we ended things, Heather. That chapter is *closed* and no, I'm not looking to reopen it. Not only that, but I've moved on and it has the potential to be something serious. Matter fact, let me correct myself, I *know* it's getting serious." I thought back to the phone call and what was said and what I had yet to fully hear. "Look, you're a great mother to our daughter and a great woman when you not on that bullshit. Give whatever dude it is that you with a real chance, especially if you claiming him. I know I'ma give what I **have** my all."

Her eyes weld up with tears but she blinked them back. "Okay, Has. I respect your decision, forreal this time. I think you've put up with enough of my shenanigans so I'm gonna do what's right and focus on what I have."

"Good. I wish you the best of luck in that. And if you're really serious, I wanna meet this nigga before you have him all up in my baby's face."

"That's fair, and the same goes for you and the car lady."

"Her name is Charisma. You gotta work on that respect thing because she demands it." I all but let her know that Charisma wasn't going for nothing strange.

"My bad, I mean, Charisma, the car lady. Have a goodnight." She smirked and started up her car.

"Yeah, get home safe and send a text once y'all made it in."

"Alright."

She pulled off and I hopped in my car. Destination? Charisma's crib to see what was going on with my future, literally.

CHAPTER THIRTEEN – CHARISMA

"Shit, shit, shit. He was on the phone the whole time. I'm sure he heard your big ass mouth, Brae'lynn!" I plopped down on my couch and put my head in my hands.

I'd just disconnected the call that I made on accident to Hasan and to say I was nervous about how much of the conversation he heard was an understatement. I was scared of his reaction which was why I had been hiding that I'd been throwing up on and off for the last two days. Even while he slept the previous night, I'd crept out of bed and into the bathroom to hurl, using the water to drown out the sounds. I got back into bed with a fresh mouth after brushing my teeth and went back to sleep. Just like I hadn't said anything to Hasan, I hadn't uttered a word about it to the girls.

Asani just so happened to come over this morning for us to talk about the property she'd shown Hasan. She'd been receiving calls with offers but had halted any further showings until Hasan put in his bid. I was confident that he'd put in one soon and excited to watch him become a full-fledged businessman.

When Asani arrived, she immediately picked up on my flushed face, but I brushed off her concern, citing that I wasn't feeling good because of something bad I'd eaten the night before. She let me slide and decided to ride with me to my mother's bakery to check in with her. We didn't make it out the house good before I was hugging the toilet and puking my guts up. Again, Asani questioned what was wrong and my answer was the same.

Entering the bakery, the smell of cake batter infiltrated my nostrils and I almost didn't make it to the bathroom, but Asani helped me along. She all but demanded that we leave the bakery and stop at the nearest pharmacy. Not wanting to raise suspicion with my mom or Hasan's mom, who just so happened to be at the bakery, I made up an excuse for our sudden need to leave. Running into Hasan on our way out threw a monkey wrench in my quick escape and when I threw up in front of him, I was *too* over it. I was even more on board to get to the pharmacy. And even though Asani had almost had word vomit, she played it off as to not worry Hasan. Now, I was wishing that I hadn't rushed because I wasn't ready for the two pink lines to show up on three different tests.

"Not you mad with me cause you butt dialed the man," Brae'lynn responded, matching my tone, and taking a seat across from me.

"Dammit!" I yelled out in frustration. "I know and I'm sorry, I just... I don't know y'all. This wasn't supposed to happen." I kept my head down and they both huddled around me.

"You're scared, boo, and that's understandable." I knew Asani's words were meant to be comforting but they didn't hit the way I'm sure she wanted them to.

"It's only been a month today, Sani. One damn month."

"And you've been fucking almost every other day for that month. Real raw dawg energy, so I'm not surprised." Sani and I both shot Brae'lynn a look and she motioned like she was zipping her lips.

"Yes, please do cause you ain't helping at all right now," Sani let her know.

"She's not," I added, "...but she's deadass right. And I do have to tell Hasan, sooner than later."

Brae'lynn raised her hand, requesting to speak.

"Something is really wrong with you," Asani said and I shook my head. "Say what you gotta say, Brae'lynn."

"Okay. I know that by *society's standards,* this is happening too fast and y'all are still in the dating stage, but if we put all of that to the side, how do you feel about Hasan?"

My heart fluttered. "I'm in *deep like* with him. He checks all of my boxes. He's patient, funny, loving, an amazing dad, he's smart, and most importantly, he's willing. Willing and open to learning new things and to learn *me*. We are compatible in so many ways and the things we may not be in sync with, we're not tryna change it in the other person. We're willing to adapt and that's important to me."

"So, what I just heard is, he's **everything** you want and the only reason why being pregnant right now is a bad idea is because of *the time* y'all have known each other."

When she said it, it sounded so trivial, but it was anything but. "Yes," I answered.

"And *that* right there is where we tend to fuck up and lose out on people and things that are sent to us for a reason. You're scared of the unknown and I get that, we all are. At the same time, I remember a year ago when we sat in this *very spot* and talked about things we wanted to accomplish and where we saw ourselves in a year. I recall you saying you wanted to be in a loving relationship where the person was their full self from the door. You also said you wanted to give school your all so that you could graduate earlier."

"Yeah, Brae'lynn, I did say that. I said nothing about a baby."

"And that's a blessing that you should consider as the cherry on top," she countered.

"Wow," Asani spoke up, "you broke that shit down, B. And I agree."

It was cool that they were on the same page, but they weren't the ones I had to make the final decision with as to what my next steps would be. That would be Hasan.

THE GIRLS HAD LEFT, GIVING ME TIME TO MYSELF TO WEIGH THE pros and cons of my current situation. I wanted to call Hasan back to feel him out but reasoned that if he did hear anything, he would've called me. In my mind I ran down so many scenarios that I ended up falling asleep on the couch. A knock on the door woke me up. Picking up my phone to check the time, it read 7:35p.m. I'd slept for some hours and missed the two calls Hasan had made to me.

"Just a minute," I called out after the person on the other side knocked again. Looking through the peephole and seeing Hasan's face, I put my head up against the door.

"I gotta talk to you through the door now?"

"I'm scared to open it," I admitted.

"Why you scared, Charisma?" His tone was soft as if he were talking to his three-year-old.

"I just am."

"I don't like that you feel that way. Open the door so I can hold you. Whatever it is that you're scared of, we'll face it together."

A lone tear fell down my face and I unlocked the door and pulled it open.

"I'm pregnant, Hasan," I blurted out before he could step into the house. There was no soft way to deliver the news.

"I figured as much."

"How?"

"This may sound crazy, but I kinda have an idea of how pregnant pussy feels. And today was the first day I witnessed you throwing up, but I heard you last night. You hopped back in the bed so fast; I knew you were hiding something but didn't wanna pressure you to tell me if you weren't ready. I also overheard your conversation when you butt dialed me." He closed the door behind himself, locked it, and pulled me to him by my wife beater. "Were you gonna tell me had you not butt dialed me? Be honest."

"I was but I had to wrap my head around it first."

"That's fair. So, what we doing?"

I shrugged. "I don't know. I didn't intend to come in your life and shake things up in this way. It's one thing to start a whole whirlwind romance with the dating and all that, but *a baby*. This shit is big, Hasan."

"I know. I have a three-year-old, remember."

"Yeah, with a woman you knew for a while before y'all conceived.

And that's another thing, adding another baby will change the current dynamics."

"Says who?" He looked down at my worry filled face and wiped my cheek.

"I don't know, says history."

"Listen," he lifted my chin and kissed my lips, "if God didn't know that you were in good hands and I didn't have good intentions, he wouldn't have placed that baby in your womb. Granted, sometimes he gives kids to some fucked up individuals but that's not the case here. If you decide we're keeping the baby, trust me when I say there's nothing in this world that would affect the way in which I show up for my children. He or she would just be an added blessing, you understand?"

"Yes." I voiced my understanding because his statement held so much conviction. "What about your shop and your other business?"

"I thought you said you understood."

"I do."

"Then what did I say?"

"Nothing in this world will affect how you show up for your children."

"Right, and add *yourself* in that sentence, too."

I took a deep breath and smiled. "I guess the decision is made then. So much for a turn up Summer."

"Girl, this was a Summer to remember. Now can I have a kiss?" I kissed him passionately and my heart fluttered, the same way it had when my eyes met his for the first time. After four chance encounters and dating for a month, we were about to take on parenthood together. We were the definition of FATE.

THE END

Did you enjoy the read?
Let us know how much by leaving us a review on Amazon and Goodreads.

"This game wasn't meant to be ran by a woman," my father told me as I sat across from him in the visiting room at San Quentin State prison. "It's male dominated just like anything else in this world and that's why you gotta be five steps ahead. You come from my loins, so you already have an advantage. I raised you to be a strong leader and never take no for an answer. Your poise and resilience will play a part in your takeover. I'm passing the baton to you and it's going to fuck up the heads of a lot of people but don't concern yourself with idle chit chat. Keep your womanly mannerisms. Just because you're the boss don't mean that you have to act like a man. Stay the course and do this shit right... the Wright way."

I took in everything he said, soaking the words up like a sponge. I knew what was being asked of me and I had no intentions on letting my father down. I had to act like a woman while thinking like a man. Stepping into the shoes of Curtis "Coolie" Wright wasn't going to be an easy feat, but my daddy didn't raise no hoe. With my Queens by my side, we were sure to shake up the city.

"I hear you, daddy. I'm gonna make sure they never forget your name. It'll be like you never left," I assured him.

"They never forget a Legend, baby girl. You just make sure they know the *new* First Lady at The Table." He reached across the metal table for my hand and squeezed it. It was a sign to let me know that he had to go. Since he started serving his sentence, we had the whole visiting thing down to a science. We never said goodbye because it was too final for me. Instead, he squeezed my hand and I'd say, "until we meet again," and he would nod his head and smile. After doing our ritual, we both stood.

"I love you, daddy."

"I love you too, daughter. Go out there and make me proud."

I sat at the head of the conference table in one of the office buildings I owned with my best friends, Tiffany and Morae to the left and right of me as we conducted the monthly money meeting for The Table. We each listened as the heads of each borough gave account of what they needed for their re-up as well as handing over our portion of their profit. Everything was going smooth until we got to Briscoe. Briscoe had control of Brooklyn. His cocky ass couldn't take the fact that *I* now ran the entire operation. It didn't help that we were ex-lovers. Since I'd been put in position, he made sure to never miss an opportunity to act like a dickhead.

"This nigga," Tiffany whispered as we watched Briscoe play on his phone as if he didn't know it was his time to report. "Ay, Briscoe, I don't know if you think the concept no longer applies to you, but time is money. And right now, you wasting it. Report, nigga," she pushed.

"Oh, it's my turn?" He played dumb. Reaching down, he picked up an MCM book bag off the floor and sat it on the table. "That's seventy bands." Morae got up and snatched the bag off the table before proceeding to the money room to count it. Like Tiffany, she was tired of his bullshit too.

Over his shenanigans and blatant disrespect, I leaned forward and folded one black, gel- manicured hand over the other before speaking. "You've wasted five minutes of my time that I can never get back. I'm gonna need you to go ahead and add five thousand to your monthly payout. That's a stack for each minute wasted." The smirk he had on his face was now gone.

"Oh, you fining niggas now over bullshit? Get the fuck outta here Mahogany. The way I'm out here bringing in money and you tryna *lil boy* me?" He stood in a threatening manner and from the corner of my eye, I could see Tiffany place her gun on the table.

"All of this huffing and puffing over five G'z, Briscoe? Damn, I'm disappointed in you, baby. I suggest you pipe the fuck down though; you know how Tiff gets when she feels I'm being disrespected." Slowly, he sat down, and I knew by the slits in his eyes he was embarrassed and pissed about it. I gave not one fuck because he had brought it on himself. "Trick, you're up."

I listened as Trick, who sat to the left of Briscoe, gave his report while Briscoe stared a hole in the side of my face. From day one, he didn't respect my position. He thought that by my father treating him like a son when we were together, he was being groomed to be next in line. He was sadly mistaken because I always knew the operation would be handed over to me if something happened to my dad. It got under his skin that he had to answer to me, a woman. I held the power for him to keep getting money in the city.

"Aight, meeting adjourned," Morae spoke after reentering the room. "Same time next month fellas. If for any reason you need to re-up earlier than your scheduled time, you know where to find me." With no further words spoken, everyone got up to make their exit. As usual, once everyone cleared out, the ladies and I debriefed. I didn't let Briscoe get by me though.

"Aye Briscoe," I called out to the angry man, "you're forgetting something." Tiffany smirked when he turned around. Digging in his pocket, he counted out fifty $100 bills and placed the blue faces on the table. I watched as he ran his tongue over his teeth before pushing the money towards me. I knew he wanted to say something but opted out of it. "Thank you, love." He nodded his head and walked out. Nobody's ever always happy with the boss.

———

"You need to let his ass go. That nigga so envious of you, it don't even make no sense," Morae said as we debriefed and put away the monthly take.

"I agree with Mo. He wants yo' position bad," Tiffany added. I knew they were right, but the only thing stopping me from cutting Briscoe off was the fact that he did bring in money--lots of it. Although he acted like a bitch behind me being over him, he hadn't snaked me on the business side. I couldn't say that I knew how long it would last though.

"I hear what y'all saying and trust me when I say I'm keeping an eye on him. Briscoe may envy me, but he knows betta than to cross me. He loves his family too much." In the Wright organization, we were big on loyalty and didn't allow second chances when it came down to it. You crossed us, we let everyone close to you feel it and leave you alive just so you could live with the fact that you were the reason for their demise.

"Look, I'll never tell you how to handle business, but I'm telling you the longer you let that nigga live with that malice in his heart, that shit is just going to fester. And that's going to be bad for business," Morae spoke again.

I looked over at her and smirked. "You just want to kill him, don't you?"

"Oh, please, please, please." She had her hands up in a praying motion while she bat her eyes. "I promise not to make it messy."

"Our friend is really looney," Tiffany joked, walking out of the vault while I shook my head and followed.

"Nuts I tell you." I laughed and Mo rolled her eyes at the both of us.

"Y'all never let me have no fun, it's cool though. And how you gon' call me looney when you practically live at the shooting range?" She closed the door behind us and locked it and I looked over at Tiff.

"Hey, I have my thing and you have yours." Tiffany shrugged her shoulders and smirked. I loved my girls. Tiffany was my God sister and we'd known Morae since we were ten. Still in our twenties, we had made a name for ourselves in the game. Morae, Tiffany, and I were three different women that bought different skillsets and personalities to The Table which enabled our business to be such a success.

Tiffany was my beautiful, head of security. With a pretty face, stacked body, and a keen sense of style, one would never peg her as anyone's protector. What people didn't know was that Tiffany was just as deadly if not deadlier than most of the killers I knew. Growing up a military kid, Tiff knew her way around guns. It wasn't uncommon for her to have us at the gun range at any given time, testing out some new shit.

Morae was head lieutenant. She ran all of our spots and ran them with an iron fist. Cold as a motherfucka too. While each borough had its HNIC, such as the guys that were gathered tonight, before anything got to my ears, it went through Mo first. She was my eyes and ears on the ground. Couldn't nobody get to me until they went through her. And even then, Mo had the answers because she knew how I was going to step at all times. A petite thing standing at 5'5, Mo had the shape of an athlete.

She stayed in the gym, toning, but maintained her feminine energy. It was likely why she attracted both women and men but preferred to play on the same team. I pondered everyday why she chose to lick cat as opposed to having a hard dick. To each's own though. More than the skillsets they brought to The Table, I knew for a fact that my bitches were some riders. They would go to war with an army behind me and I knew I didn't have to question the love or loyalty they had for me.

The game was treacherous, and in order to survive in it, you had to have people who were gonna step behind you, no questions asked. I had that times two, well three if you included my father. Shit, even behind the wall, if Coolie wanted you touched, you got touched. Those bars didn't mean shit. As for me, I was the team's all-around player, keeping things running like a well-oiled machine in the background.

To the world, I was Mahogany Wright, the woman behind the infamous "Elite Palace." A popular gentlemen's club in Westchester, NY. I had the baddest bitches, and the niggas came from far and wide to be a part of the "Elite Experience." There was something for everybody at Elite, though. We didn't just cater to the men.

While I had a host of beautiful women who worked in my club, my premiere dancers made it so that it was the talk of the city. Cherokee, Bad Ass Bri, Kat, and Paris were handpicked by me and Morae. We'd done a good job because not only did they make the niggas spend bands, but they were also trained to kill any motherfucka that was a threat. I ran my club just as I'd run The Table in many ways, with a strict no bullshit policy. I didn't allow drugs in my establishment unless I was the one supplying them, and it was never anything hard. I supplied edibles and free hookah. If you wanted a different high, you could purchase any exotic weed of your choosing or X.

"Are you going into the club tonight?" Mo asked as we walked to our cars. Daylight savings had rolled around, and it was darker than usual for it to only be eight o'clock.

"Not tonight. I promised Beautii I'd be home after this meeting. She wants me to take her out to dinner, said she needs to talk to me."

"If Beautii don't go head," Tiffany laughed. "My girl wanna talk over dinner. I swear she is you all day." It was true, my nine-year-old daughter was a mini me. She had my face and my mannerisms down to a T.

"Yeah, that's my baby so you know I gotta make it happen. What y'all getting into?" Using my remote starter to start my Porsche Cayenne Coupe, I walked around the driver's side to get in.

"After I make sure you get home, I'm gonna take it in for the night. I don't feel like being around a crowd and you know tomorrow is brunch with my dad. I gotta be up and before time."

"And alert," I reminded Tiffany.

"As fuck. You know he don't give a bitch a break. What about you, Mo?" Tiffany asked Morae whose head was in her phone. "Mo!" Tiff yelled out to get her attention.

Mo's eyes shot up and annoyance was written all over her face. "You ain't have to do all that. And yeah, I'm gonna swing by the club a little later to see Paris."

I smirked, opening my door to put my purse inside. "You are smitten by that girl."

"I ain't smitten by nobody. I do fuck with her heavy though," she called herself correcting me.

"Girl, that is just the hood definition of smitten." We all shared a laugh, and she waved me off.

"I'll hit the chat once I make it to the club," she said and went to hop in her car. Beeping the horn twice once she started it up, she drove off into the night.

I didn't mind Mo dating one of my dancers because we had long ago set boundaries. She knew she couldn't hoard Paris when she was on the clock and there was no PDA on the floor. I was big on not mixing business with pleasure and Mo respected that. I also lead by example which was why I made sure to separate how I felt about Briscoe from the business.

"You ready?" Tiffany nodded towards me.

"Yeah." I climbed into my car and connected to my Bluetooth to call Beautii.

"Hey, mommy," she answered, not letting the call ring fully.

"Hey, sugar, were you waiting by the phone?"

"Yep. Are you on your way home?"

I smiled and shook my head. **"I am, so you can start getting dressed. Where's Gran?"** I asked about my mother.

"In the kitchen, reading."

"Okay, I'll see you in a minute. Be dressed when I come through the door, Beautii."

"I will. Love you, mommy."

"I love you too, my girl." Ending the call just as Tiff pulled up next to me, I rolled down my window.

"You down to put some speed on yo' baby tonight?" She was referring to my car. We had pulled up to the meeting in the same car and cracked up at the coincidence.

"Not tonight, Tiff. Let's just get home."

"Ahh, okay. I knew you was scared I was gon' dust yo' ass. Go head and pull out, I'm right behind you."

I smirked and gave her the finger. Truth was, I didn't feel like racing because the girls' comments were on my mind. Briscoe was showing his ass and the last thing I was gonna tolerate was him thinking he was above The Table. I'd hate to have to put my daughter's father under it.

Available Now

On all online retail book platforms!!

OTHER BOOKS BY

URBAN AINT DEAD

Tales 4rm Da Dale
By **Elijah R. Freeman**

The Hottest Summer Ever
By **Elijah R. Freeman**

Despite The Odds
By **Juhnell Morgan**

Good Girl Gone Rouge
By **Manny Black**

Hittaz 1, 2 & 3
By **Lou Garden Price, Sr.**

Charge It To The Game 1 & 2
By **Nai**

A Setup For Revenge
By **Ashley Williams**

Ridin' For You
By **Telia Teanna**

The State's Witness 1 & 2
By **Kyiris Ashley**

Stuck In The Trenches

By **Huff Tha Great**

The Swipe

By **Toola**

Coming Soon From

URBAN AINT DEAD

The Hottest Summer Ever 2

By **Elijah R. Freeman**

THE G-CODE

By **Elijah R. Freeman**

How To Publish A Book From Prison

By **Elijah R. Freeman**

Tales 4rm Da Dale 2

By **Elijah R. Freeman**

Hittaz 4

By **Lou Garden Price, Sr.**

Good Girl Gone Rouge 2

By **Manny Black**

Despite The Odds 2

By **Juhnell Morgan**

Charge It To The Game 3

By **Nai**

The State's Witness 3

By **Kyiris Ashley**

Ridin For You, Too

By **Telia**

Stuck In The Trenches 2

By **Huff That Great**

A Setup For Revenge 2

By **Ashley Williams**

The Swipe 2

By **Toola**

BOOKS BY

URBAN AINT DEAD's C.E.O

<u>Elijah R. Freeman</u>

Triggadale 1, 2 & 3

Tales 4rm Da Dale

The Hottest Summer Ever

Murda Was The Case 1 & 2

Follow
Elijah R. Freeman
On Social Media

FB: Elijah R. Freeman

IG: @the_future_of_urban_fiction